WEAPONS OF MASS DELUSION
America's *Real* National Emergency

Richard Forno

Copyright 2003 by Richard Forno. All Rights Reserved.

www.rickonline.org

All rights reserved. No part of this publication may be reproduced or transmitted in any form or by any means electronic or mechanical, including photocopy, recording, or any information storage and retrieval system, without permission in writing from the copyright owner.

Published by Potomac View Books
Arlington, VA

Cover Design by Matt Fendahleen <matt@fendahleen.com>

ISBN 1-58961-111-X
Printed in the United States of America

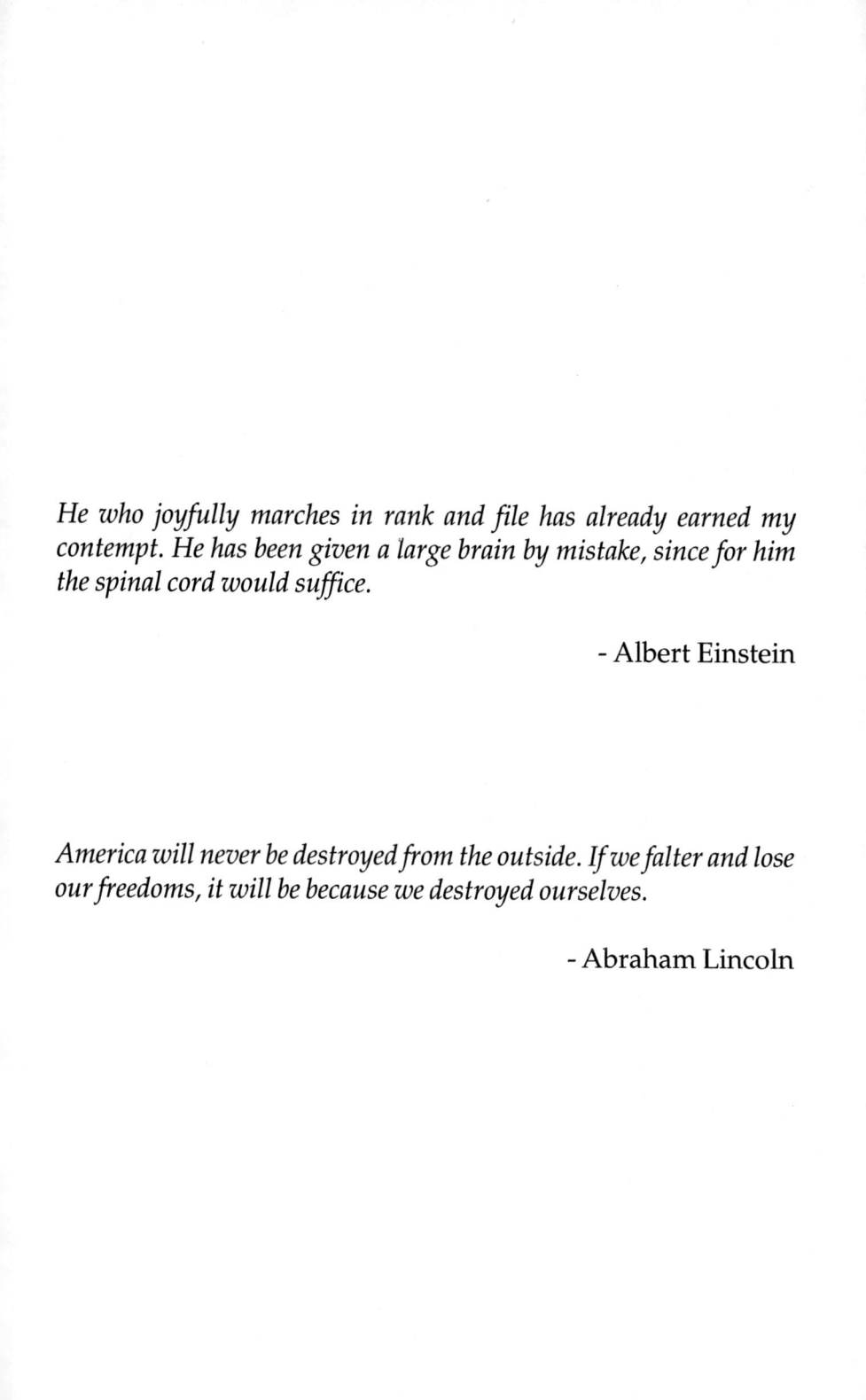

He who joyfully marches in rank and file has already earned my contempt. He has been given a large brain by mistake, since for him the spinal cord would suffice.

- Albert Einstein

America will never be destroyed from the outside. If we falter and lose our freedoms, it will be because we destroyed ourselves.

- Abraham Lincoln

Acknowledgements

This product of cultural exploration didn't come about in a vacuum, but with the advice, counsel, sympathetic shoulders, and good old-fashioned help of friends and family with a diverse range of political, religious, and social views.

Special thanks (and autographed copies) go to Jay Dyson, Robert Ferrell, Richard Thieme, Raven Alder, Brian Martin, Bill Feinbloom, Alison Pacuska, A.J. Morning, Jeff Christoph, and Dr. Emilie Sair for their advice, counsel, and assistance as this book came together. To those who aren't named for one reason or other, I thank you sincerely as well.

Words alone can't express my gratitude to Dr. Elyn Wollensky — a wonderful, intelligent friend and keen editor — who somehow managed to fit me into her schedule and help transform my initial (and quite emotional) rants into something considerably more readable, balanced, and less angst-filled, often doing so in the wee hours of the night and over the phone. I'm not sure how I can repay her fully, but I'm going to try.

Additional thanks go to the Wachowski brothers for their 1999 cinematic message (*The Matrix*) that inspired me to write this book and help distribute Red Pills to the American public. Art is sometimes a chilling reflection on reality, and it's a shame more people can't see beyond the action and special effects wizardry to glean valuable insights on the real world.

Finally, most loving thanks to my close friends, fondly-remembered teachers and family, by whose words, deeds, examples, support, and sacrifices I've become a stronger and more enlightened person, adult, and American. You're all a treasured part of me.

To the independently-minded thinkers, journalists, authors, analysts, lecturers, teachers, citizens, and rare public officials who hold fast to their principles and intellects by steadfastly refusing to surrender either despite the overwhelming (and sometimes very enticing) special-interest machinations polluting our society today.

In other words, this book is dedicated to all who can, and do, think and act for themselves.

Table of Contents

Preface 11
The Realist Manifesto 16
Democracy Lives — But Where Are The People? 26
Spinning the Body Politic... 39
Why Stop the Buck, When You Can Pass It? 54
Newsporn 59
Regarding Political Correctness in Schools 67
Schoolyard Stalag 73
Cloistered Kids Syndrome 79
Functional Illiterates 85
Generation Rx 93
God, Inc. 98
Interpreting the Ten Commandments in 2003 107
The Christian Wrong 113
America's Profitable Red Light Districts 124
Homeland Insecurity 130
The Terror Alert They Won't Issue 141
The New Normal 148
Greed Respects No Tragedy 153
The Approaching Digital Dark Ages 156
Hollywood's War for Social Control................................. 163
Empowering America the Right Way 171
Afterward – July 2003 179
Endnotes 188

Preface

In the end they will lay their freedom at our feet and say to us, 'Make us your slaves, but feed us.'
-Dostoevsky's *Grand Inquisitor*.

The desire to write this book came about during the latter part of the Dot Com Days; when cash flowed freely, lavish parties were held nightly for start-ups not yet formed, business plans submitted on cocktail napkins received significant venture funding, and multi-million-dollar IPOs were deemed the perfect end to a business plan.

In those heady days, Americans were overwhelmed with any number of technologically-enabled ways to free themselves and become enlightened members of the global society.

Technology was supposed to be the cause of our enlightenment, and we happily embraced it without a second thought. It was cool, it was neat and, like good sex, it felt really warm and wonderful — and all we wanted was more.

Faster, better, and cheaper was the way of life, and little else seemed to matter.

In some ways it was the 1960s all over — only thirty years later with slicker marketing and better hygiene. This time, the drug of choice was a double-shot of caffeine instead of a (hopefully) strychnine-free paper tab of LSD. Peace, love, and rock-and-roll were replaced with high-tech, venture capital, and IPO. The Love Generation became the Era of Instant Gratification.

But working in the heart of the Dot Com apex, I began to notice cracks in the facade of our new American enlightenment. Eventually, I realized that despite the hype, free-flowing money, and few real benefits of the Dot Com era, it was all a giant illusion — and some might even call it a *mass delusion*. The problem wasn't just that the emperor was naked; this time there wasn't a castle, a kingdom, or even an emperor!

In other words, this delusion hid serious problems that needed addressing in our national reality.

Reality was that for over two hundred years, America's citizens — and this means the average individual, not just large donors, heads of corporations and party affiliates, despite what you might believe — were active, vocal, critical members of America's governing body. Citizens served as jurists and citizen-administrators in their government. They flocked to the polls on Election Day to make educated, conscientious decisions about who they wanted to represent them in the halls of local and national governments. As patriots, they volunteered when called upon, and stayed informed on the issues of the day. They cared about their community and country. They were *citizens*. They were Americans interested in the betterment of their nation in the years to come.

But that was then.

Today's New American Reality is that despite, or perhaps due to, the technological innovations of the Dot Com years, America devolved into a nation of individual customers and consumers interested only in the here-and-now affairs of their society but not its future. Some might even argue this process has been happening for decades, and was only accelerated by the free-flowing capital of the now-extinct Dot Com years; but regardless, it's still an Era of Instant Gratification only looking at the Here and Now.

You see, *citizens* are united by common interests and a desire to improve their communities; *customers* are a group of like-minded individuals looking for the best service at the best rate. And even if they receive courteous service and deep discounts, customers will never own the store and really don't care who provides the services as long as they can get them affordably when they need — or want — them. While yesterday's citizens owned their government, today's customers simply pay to receive services from it — and whether they're getting their money's worth from taxes paid is the subject for a whole other book.

In other words, taking a cue from today's world of faster, better, and cheaper, we've learned to handle personal and social problems in the same way we handle a computer problem: find a quick fix at a good price. Let the elected officials and paid-for-helpers handle problems that crop up in life — after all, that's what they're being paid to worry about so we don't have to.

However, these technologically-enlightened members of the global society — who can proudly access 600 channels of cable television while reading about breaking news and celebrity gossip across the Internet and talking to their friends across the country with no roaming or long-distance charges from their super-sized suburban McMansions or two-foot-per-gallon SUVs — need to think again. We forget that, as Goethe wrote over two hundred years ago, "none are more hopelessly enslaved than those who falsely believe they are free."

To break this down into easy to understand consumer-speak, the ability to buy lots and lots of stuff on credit and access tons of interesting-but-useless information does not make a person free no matter what the commercials and politicians seem to promise. Neither does having an infatuation with pop culture and an ignorance of current affairs or the world around us. Even our ability to make a difference by exercising the right to vote has diminished seriously in recent years given our abysmal voter turnout at election time.

For governments, religions, and corporations — the accepted entities of social control — this is an easy environment to maintain dominance over, especially given the collective ignorance of an American public that is unable or perhaps unwilling to acknowledge its true reality and take steps to improve it for themselves.

Real patriots don't ask questions, and normal people don't challenge the status quo — at least that's what we're led to believe, especially after September 2001. Besides, we're too busy trying to live up to the promises and visions of being free that we just don't have the time or inclination to worry about such things. Real patriots just do what they're told. So do sheep.

Yet we still believe we're free, and accept whatever we're given in return for relinquishing our independence to people who — once elected — cater more to wealthy contributors and devious special interests than the individual voters who elected them. In other words, we're outsourcing (or possibly already *outsourced*) the very democratic ideals we Americans purportedly cherish.

This book suggests that the America of 2003 is built not on citizens, but on sheep-like consumer-subjects existing in a world of social and intellectual bondage — because as soon as we allowed these organizations to start thinking and acting on our behalf, it wasn't *our* America any more — it became *theirs*. And it is theirs right now.

Let's look at a few examples of this New American Reality in action. We believe that personal privacy is important, yet routinely allow corporate and political interests to whittle them away without a second thought. We believe in the separation of religion from government as a fundamental American principle, yet continue to tolerate religion's deepening influence in the development of national laws and policies. We brought the world into the Information Age, yet have an embarrassing national literacy rate and a horrific public education system. We blindly trust the latest technology without thinking about what we're sacrificing for its convenience. We clamor daily about our constitutional rights, but few have ever read the Constitution to learn what rights and protections they're entitled to as citizens. These problems — and others discussed in this book — help establish an American society that is unable to think for (or help) itself and content to live in a world of blissful ignorance where mindlessly going along with the herd is not only expected but the best most can hope to achieve in their lifetime, even though we're capable of so much more as people and a society.

The real national emergency facing America in 2003 isn't terrorism or weapons of mass destruction; it's what we are allowing ourselves to become. Living an illusion and being part of a mass delusion may be comfortable, easy, and feel good, but in the end we're only hurting ourselves. The reality is that we don't need to go overseas to find weapons of mass destruction, we've got a much more dangerous stockpile of *weapons of mass delusion* right here at home to worry about.

This book contains observations and opinions that you may or may not agree with. I'm not saying they're right or wrong, just that they're mine. But if even some of what you read gets you thinking differently about our society and perhaps motivates you to help make it a better one somehow, then as its author, I've accomplished what I set out to do. The bottom line is that I've got my opinions, and you've got yours. You're reading mine now, and I'll respect yours later.

It's high time we stepped up to the challenge of accepting responsibility for ourselves by acknowledging the problems we're uncomfortable talking about and taking the necessary steps to remedy them, if for no other reason than to figure out how to build a better, more secure, and stable America for our posterity. And if we're lucky, maybe we'll be able to improve things for ourselves along the way.

RICHARD FORNO
Washington, DC

1

The Realist Manifesto

Facts do not cease to exist just because they are ignored.
-Aldous Huxley

Though this book is one-third pop culture, one-third social science and one-third satire, it can be seen as one-hundred-percent political. Because of this, I will present my political beliefs up-front so that there is no confusion about who I am and what I stand for.

To begin with, I love America. I love the principles this nation was founded on; and while we have our fair share of problems and embarrassments (discussed in this book) we also have a lot to be proud of and defend.

Earlier in life, I called myself a "Republican" — but as I studied and gained a deeper understanding of the country and world, I was no longer able to identify simply with just one party and its platform, especially since being associated with a single party implies you support *everything* that party stands for, which it shouldn't. For example, it's hard to call yourself a Republican if you support a woman's right to have an abortion, and it's hard to call yourself a Democrat if you support something that remotely resembles a tax credit. As such, my current views range from the social-centric interests of the Democrats to the strong-military interests of the Republicans. You could say that I'm somewhere in the middle.

Yet I will not call myself a "centrist." With both the Republicans and Democrats gravitating inwards to reach the undecided voters in recent years, being a centrist has lost all real significance as it becomes polluted by these dueling factions fishing for new sheep...er, members.

So how do I classify myself? I've thought about what I find right and wrong in America today — about what I agree with in party platforms and what I disagree with. I've read the Constitution and the Bill of Rights — and many of the laws being passed or proposed today by the American mainstream political machine. At the end of the day, I have formed my own opinions — based on ideals and principles I was taught at home, in school, and by the examples of those whom I admire. The GOP (the Greed, Oil, and Power Party, otherwise known as Republicans) may say I'm a social-left-leaning liberal revisionist. Democrats, if they ever get their party's message unified, will probably find some of my views unnerving, too. And that's fine.

Because of this I call myself a Realist — and this is my Manifesto:

I am a Realist. I live my life based on reality, not wishful thinking, hyperbole, spin, empty promises, fear mongering, or adherence to a single party platform. I will not subscribe to a single "party line," and most importantly, I pride myself on routinely doing a very contemporary un-American thing by *thinking for myself and forming my own opinions* on the issues impacting on my life and nation.

I say this because:

- I believe that peacefully speaking up in protest against changes to our constitutional rights — or even quoting the Constitution — should not make someone a "person of interest" to federal law enforcement, and that questioning a position taken by whichever party is, at the moment, in power, should not label someone as "unpatriotic," "liberal," a "revisionist," or a "supporter of terrorism" in the words of government officials and the media.

- I believe the separation of governmental powers helps ensure the checks-and-balances system and can prevent a runaway government with both excessive powers and the ability to abuse those powers if it so desires. I don't believe that, with the executive, judicial and legislative branches controlled by the same political party, there will be any true government oversight or reform, let alone meaningful public debate on issues of national importance.

- With the exception of specific national security programs, I believe in the open, public accountability of government policies, programs, and expenditures to ensure that our tax dollars are spent appropriately, and that domestic political posturing isn't the primary unspoken reason for crafting or modifying America's domestic and international policies.

- I believe that the friendly-sounding "First Amendment Zones" established near today's highly-scripted political events, are intended to falsely imply public support for national policies by keeping dissenting opinion away from the president and major media coverage. I tremble when I hear that people desiring to "commit an act of free speech" at such events are restricted to areas under police surveillance, threatened with being arrested on trumped-up charges, or placed on a list as a "potential terrorist" simply for speaking their minds peacefully, as it reminds me of how police states are formed.

- I believe in the separation between all religions and government, and that "faith-based" government programs are contrary to American law and tradition. That being said, "faith" in a free nation should mean *any* religion, not simply "mainstream" religions with significant political lobbying power, or the religion of those who happen to hold elected office.

- I believe that the President should not appoint science advisors based on their religious beliefs — and that information guiding national science or medical advice and policy should be based in objective fact, not on a certain religious mythology that panders to political supporters.

- I believe that career federal prosecutors and judges should be appointed not for their political or religious views, but on how objectively they interpret America's laws to ensure that justice is applied equally to persons of all sexes and sexual orientations, faiths, political beliefs, and ethnicities.

- I believe that children must not be automatically promoted through America's educational system, and that a person's education is proven not by receiving a diploma but by demonstrating competency in certain basic skills and subjects.

- I believe that America's public education system should be drastically improved: teachers' unions and malfunctioning boards of education should be brought under control and forced to be accountable, instead of continuing to fund alternatives to problem school systems without ever correcting them.

- I believe that the United States should have a national health insurance system so that everyone has equal access to comprehensive and effective health care like many other industrialized nations.

- I believe that government research reports such as projected employment (or mass layoff) statistics and environmental quality must remain available to the public and not be altered by an administration, even if such figures run contrary to the rosy picture an administration wishes to present to the American people. The American taxpayer deserves to see truthful, unbiased reports on the issues and concerns that matter to them and their nation, especially if they're footing the bill.

- I believe that the concept of "family" can mean more than just the union of a man and a woman in marriage, and that "family values" is nothing more than a marketing term used by the Religious Right to proselytize their beliefs and "morally-cleanse" our country.

- I believe that women are entitled to retain full control over their bodies, and that religious dogma shouldn't govern their independent human right of self-determination.

- I believe that more gun control laws aren't needed if the existing ones aren't being enforced properly yet, and that — contrary to popular opinion — guns, like nearly everything else, don't kill people by themselves.

- I believe in a strong national military that is prepared for future contingencies and treats its members as professionals, not social experiments. Likewise, I want our national security strategy and the development of new weapons systems to be based on real threats facing the nation and not on the interests of America's military-industrial establishment or incumbent politicians trying to stay in office by catering to their special interests.

- I want to know the truth about any national energy plan that continues to be withheld vigorously from the public for no other evident reason than to avoid possible political embarrassment or criminal admission.

- I believe that a true declaration of war is not the president's to make, but a function of the Congress as stipulated by the Constitution we cherish. Further, when such a declaration is made, it's done for legitimate reasons that are made completely public and don't change weekly to fit the political mood of the nation.

- I don't believe that declaring a "war" on an intangible concept such as terrorism, AIDS, poverty, or drugs is anything other than a political publicity stunt, and that we certainly won't ever "win" against whatever it is we're allegedly "fighting" for. However, I do believe that declaring a "war" on a tangible target such as al-Qaeda or the Taliban is an achievable (and necessary) goal, provided it is conducted in a direct, effective manner by those assets most qualified to achieve victory.

- I don't believe a national leader should tell the nation's adversaries to "bring it on" and essentially invite them to attack America's troops in the field. Doing so is not only unprofessional and undignified for a diplomat, but tells the troops that their lives don't matter as long as their swaggering Cowpoke-in-Chief can look tough on camera going into election season. It's also quite juvenile.

- I don't think it's politically- or socially-acceptable for a president to refuse to speak on a major policy issue at a public event unless he's guaranteed a standing ovation and nothing but "adulation and praise" from those attending.[1] Such desires to manipulate public perception is reminiscent of the staged political rallies found in Nazi Germany or the Soviet Union.

- I don't feel that the yellow press (which includes television news) has the authority to declare the winners of any election until the polls close and the actual votes are counted. I also don't feel that a close relative of a candidate or a campaign chairperson should be involved in a role that could present an image of election tampering to the casual observer.

- I don't believe that television news programs speak for all Americans, but I do believe that all commercial news programs "spin" faster than gyroscopes despite their claims to the contrary — particularly since they are for-profit entities driven by finicky advertisers afraid of offending anyone.

- I believe in hiring the right person for the right job, regardless of race, color, creed, sex, or political views. Being forced – or desiring – to hire someone simply to demonstrate a "commitment to diversity and affirmative action" (or for public perception value) tells me that politics, not getting the job done properly and effectively by the most-qualified candidate, is the primary concern of the hiring manager.

- I don't believe in government handouts; if you're poor, *no* job is beneath you. You may not like what you're doing at the moment, but how long you stay in that job depends on how well *you* perform and create additional opportunities for yourself to advance into a better position. The same goes for any industry that continually beseeches the government for bailouts due to poor management decisions. Being content to sit back and wait for (or expect) government handouts is the mark of a lazy person and an irresponsible organization.

- I don't think it's appropriate for the media to rewrite history by removing images of the now-fallen World Trade Center towers from pre-2001 television shows and movies. Trying to forget those structures — or the attack — may feel good in the short term, but it dishonors those who perished and glosses over a major turning point in American history.

- I don't believe it is ethically or morally correct to foster a continuing climate of fear in America in order to gain public approval for questionable military and legal ventures at home and abroad, especially while other critical domestic policies such as education and the economy are ignored, and thousands of Americans are now panicked about their retirement security after the burst of the Dot Com Bubble in 2000.

- I believe that secret tribunals, no-warrant searches, denial of due process, disregarding the directives of federal judges, obsessive surveillance, and other new "anti-terrorism" activities (such as the anything-but-patriotic-except-in-name "USA-PATRIOT Act") that gut the Constitution are criminal, and if the implications of these new make-them-up-as-we-go-along government powers are ever fully understood by the average American, they would be challenged instantly.

- I question the legitimacy of appointing as Attorney General someone known to have racist tendencies, Orwellian delusions, extremist religious views, and who — as an indication of his popularity — lost a Senate race to a dead man.

- I question why America's leaders always close public speeches with "God bless America." Not that we don't need help from a deity of some sort, but doesn't this sort of imply that we think the Christian religion of America (and it's view of "God") is better than someone else's religion and deity? Religious beliefs are highly personal and vary around the world — I say it's better to keep religion out of politics rather than invite, instigate, or imply a holy war.

- I believe that the only true symbol of the United States is the Constitution, not the flag or the dollar.

- I believe that federal holidays — especially Memorial Day and Independence Day — should be revered for their national significance and not for the deep discounts at malls and automobile dealerships offered on those days.

- I believe that if a state offers "Choose Life" license plates to those opposing abortion, it should offer "Women's Rights" license plates for those supporting a woman's right to choose. Otherwise, it's a one-sided politico-religious statement that strongly suggests religious involvement with government policies.

- I think it's unconscionable to pay a professional sports player $100 million for a multi-year contract when teachers, nurses, small-town doctors, and other social service professionals are forced to do "more with less" and use their generally meager salaries to support work-related expenses.

- I believe that the more flags one displays or wears is not an indicator that one is a better patriot or person. What people do to help their fellow citizens and/or those in-need is a much better indicator of their national pride and level of compassion as a human being and citizen.

I'm a Realist, and this is my Manifesto.

2

Democracy Lives, But Where Are The People?

Give the people contests they win by remembering the words to more popular songs.... don't give them slippery stuff like philosophy or sociology to tie things up with. That way lies melancholy...
- Fire Captain Beatty, discussing political strategy in Ray Bradbury's *Fahrenheit 451*

Whenever I watch the "Tonight Show" I cringe when Jay Leno hits the Los Angeles sidewalks to ask the average person-on-the-street elementary school questions and they nervously giggle trying to answer correctly.[2] Even though Leno only airs the interviews where folks *don't* know things, you'd think a grown adult — let alone a college student — would know (for example) that Asia isn't in the Western Hemisphere or that there are fifty stars and thirteen stripes on the American flag.

Asking elementary questions to the average American and watching them struggle with the answer isn't comedy. It's embarrassment. People shouldn't laugh at such fundamental ignorance or feel comfortable doing so — they should be ashamed.

The hard truth is that most Americans are not only apathetic and seriously uninformed, but lack a fundamental understanding of how their country works — or should work — let alone the rest of the world, or even know where to look and find such things out for themselves. They shy away from interest in national affairs — terrorism and taxes aside — and generally content to live their lives in blissful ignorance.

But what should we expect from a nation that places self-satisfaction, money, and the knowledge of pop culture far above education as a national or personal priority? I'm convinced that Americans know significantly more about the Three Stooges than the three branches of their own government, something I fear that speaks volumes about where we're heading as an American society.

For example, *less than half* of American adults polled by the National Science Foundation during the mid-1990s knew that it takes the earth one year to orbit the sun, and that seventy-one percent of those polled didn't know what DNA was, even though they couldn't live without it.[3] (One wonders if those numbers decreased after DNA took center stage during the farcical O.J. Simpson trial that commandeered the news media back then.)

Based on these findings, I'm willing to bet that half, if not more, of all Americans don't know who their elected congressmen and senators are until it's election time and the campaign literature starts arriving in the mail.

Consider the statistical evidence of public ignorance rampant in American society. A January 2002 Gallup poll[4] showed that the majority of Americans could quickly identify the host of the game show *"Who Wants To Be A Millionaire"* (Regis Philbin) but under ten percent could identify the Speaker of the House of Representatives (Dennis Hastert) and the next in-line to be President after Dick "Dogs of War" Cheney. Dollars to doughnuts that Americans can recognize Judge Judy, Judge Brown, or any other made-for-television judge on sight, but not the Chief Justice of the Supreme Court, William Rehnquist.

So is it any wonder that the government bows solely to the interests of Fortune 500 corporations and their CEOs who lead politicians and their parties around with enticements and huge donations? These are the only people left with the quality private school education, and years of expensive Madison Avenue know-how to coax, cajole, and otherwise manipulate the mind of the public to get *their* person elected in the first place! They've realized the average, apathetic American wants to be led, entertained, and offered pie-in-the-sky fantasies of a better tomorrow but doesn't want to work to reach that goal. They are the shepards for the masses of sheep living in American society.

Obviously, the solution must be to boost education spending, clean up public schools, and process more young people through college to solve this national problem. Only then will Americans become more educated and capable citizens.

Yeah, right.

A 2000 study[5] by the American Council of Trustees and Alumni (ACTA) found that 81 percent of seniors at the nation's top fifty-five *colleges* scored a D or F on high-school level history exams. Only half of those surveyed could identify George Washington with the phrase "first in war, first in peace, first in the hearts of his countrymen," and only half knew that President Washington's Farewell Address warned against permanent alliances with foreign governments, an admonition quite relevant to America's national security today. More than one-third of the students polled were clueless about the division of power set forth in the U.S. Constitution, and barely one-quarter recognized popular excerpts from Lincoln's Gettysburg Address.

Yet, it's not *all* bad. Almost one hundred percent of graduating college students could identify MTV cartoon figures Beavis and Butthead, rapper Snoop Dog and similar pop-culture icons. If Beavis ever runs for office, he'll win by a landslide, and he knows it.

A November 2002 poll[6] of Americans between 18 and 24 conducted by the National Geographic Society showed that thirty percent of those surveyed couldn't locate the Pacific Ocean (the world's largest body of water) — and over ten percent couldn't identify their home country (the United States!) on a map.

Indeed, colleges are doing a wonderful job preparing our young for adult life, particularly if they're planning on careers in pop culture or as professional focus group subjects. They could certainly survive as welfare recipients or freeloaders. But as knowledgeable Americans or capable adults? Not really.

Even in matters of basic civics and government, Americans are woefully clueless. The 2000 ACTA study showed that sixty percent of Americans think that the president, not Congress, can declare war under the Constitution (nope!) And forty percent think the president can adjourn Congress or suspend the Constitution at will (nope, even though he might like to.) It showed that while most Americans don't know how federal judges are appointed (confirmed by the Senate,) they willingly agree to let them preside over criminal trials, interpret laws, and dispense punishments.

Learning how the nation worked was the traditional function of civics programs in school; learning about how bills become laws, presidents get elected, and how America's interpretation of democracy was intended to work, in addition to fostering student awareness and debates on assorted public issues. But today's civics courses generally are politically-correct community-service and volunteerism-oriented programs that focus on instant gratification to address the short-term symptoms[7] instead of the long-term causes of (and possible solutions to) various social ills.

As a result, the intellectual capability of the American public to hold its government accountable is practically non-existent. After all, do you really think that — despite its claims — it's in the government's best interest to produce knowledgeable citizens who one day might challenge the cozy status quo enjoyed by "the establishment?" I think not.

This lack of political awareness in America makes it easier for special interests to press their own political agendas and replace the needs of citizens with the needs of their all-mighty stockholders and board members. Since most voters don't follow politics, or are simply ignorant about what most politicians have actually voted for and said while in office, or even what political action committees (PACs) and special interests have contributed to their campaigns, they continue electing officials not on what they stand for, but on such deeply mitigating factors as who looks better, who seems nicer, who promises more, whose advertisements and television ads appeal to them and, occasionally, who their union boss tell then to vote for. And when all else fails, the average American elects to stay home and not vote, since they feel they don't matter.

And for most Americans, if something sounds good and repeated often enough, it's good enough to be accepted as fact. Just ask any marketing executive.

As a result of this collective ignorance — caused partially by our being selectively informed — America can make or break international treaties and domestic policies that the average person doesn't know about but should – because it affects them or the country, and how other nations view America. For instance, few Americans know how much our attempts to implement a pie-in-the-sky national missile defense program infuriated our international friends and created tension among our allies[8], or understand the basic international issues involved in America's "war" on terror – and why so many of our allies seem to be so upset with us on this issue despite their overt solidarity with us in the weeks following September 11.

Yet, although Americans have the constitutionally-granted ability under law to vote someone out of office, voters rarely are capable of doing so — or even holding them accountable for their actions — because they don't stay informed, or care enough to find out, let alone know how the process is done. Thus, the boat never gets rocked, bad policies and bad people stay in power, and special interests continue to dominate the legislative agenda and hold a dominant position in Washington. American governance continues on autopilot and the public relations strategy is simple: deny any facts except those presented by the administration as the absolute "truth." Thus, the cycle of public ignorance continues, and anyone attempting to apply the demands of logic to America's policy decisions is made to appear unpatriotic, especially since September 11.

So, since schooling won't help fix this problem much, the answer to this national problem must be to start watching the news regularly to become a more informed citizen, right? After all, the large networks profess their utility to the public as a trusted, fair, objective voice of the people to keep them informed. News networks produced trusted journalists like Edward Murrow, David Brinkley, and Walter Cronkite, so certainly we can trust today's news organizations and their journalists, like our parents did, right?

But *should* we?

It seems that educating the public by objective news reporting isn't the primary purpose of the programming offered by the news stations and major networks as it was in years past. Rather, the goal of today's news organizations is to keep Americans from ascertaining facts other than those carefully filtered and packaged by the networks and their sponsors to ensure network profitability. Of course, keeping the government happy helps, too.

As former CNN anchor Bernard Shaw told the *Atlanta Journal-Constitution* in a December 2002 interview[9], "you [viewers] are only getting what the government wants you to get [from major news organizations.]" He noted that viewers should listen, read and watch the news cautiously, and always be aware of what he described "confusion, haste, propaganda, and the outright use of the media." In other words, most of the news originating from Washington these days originates within the government in the form of "leaks" that preemptively spin stories a certain way before they're dinner-table discussions that might oppose the administration's message-of-the-day.

For example, ABC journalist Sheila MacVicar noted that during the 1991 war with Iraq, the Pentagon dazzled the American public with daily images from military briefings depicting a modern, high-tech war using very accurate precision-based weapons. As expected, the American people accepted what they were shown as absolute truth and demonstrative of America's superior military might in the world. Years later, however, a General Accounting Office (GAO) report showed that the Pentagon drastically oversold the effectiveness of such weapons in its much-hyped press briefings. In fact, "smart bombs" accounted for only *eight* percent of the total munitions dropped on Iraq, yet they accounted for over *eighty* percent of the cost of aerial munitions for the war[10] and nearly *all* of the televised footage shown over and over during and after the war.

In retrospect, Desert Storm wasn't as high-tech as we were led to believe at the time — a bitter fact exacerbated by knowing that few (if any) journalists covering the war questioned whatever facts the Pentagon was reporting as accurate. Only when the GAO began to investigate the issue in the ensuing years did the facts become clear and were subsequently reported by the media.

Why did this happen?

The answer is simple: Many mainstream journalists avoid asking the tough questions or digging too deeply beyond what's presented by government officials for fear of being kept "out of the loop" on future stories and thus potentially damaging their careers when they discover something potentially embarrassing yet newsworthy. As a result, there is little pressure to do more than serve as a mouthpiece for the government's message-of-the-day, something that makes for little diversity of opinion and critical analysis when reporting newsworthy items, especially in the era of a shrinking number of competing mainstream news outlets. Or, as Matthew Engel reported in a January 2003 article for the UK *Guardian*, "the supposedly liberal American press has become a dog that never bites and hardly barks but really loves rolling over and having its tummy tickled."[11]

Yet these are the same news organizations that continue to promote their image as noble servants of the public interest. Just look and see how frequently networks proclaim their status as "fair and balanced" or the "most trusted news source in America" or "the network America trusts for news" for examples of this selfless — and grossly misleading — self-promotion. As famed *Washington Post* Watergate reporter Carl Bernstein told a Florida audience in early 2003, "our [journalism's] stake in maintaining the myth and the attendant self-image that we are doing a great job is every bit as great a fiction as that of the American Congress serving the people. The gravest threat to the truth today may well be within our own profession."[12]

I think he's onto something here.

If in doubt, think at the combat coverage by the media during Operation IRAQI FREEDOM in 2003. No, not the Pentagon-hyped "shock and awe" military campaign with embedded journalists and bombs falling in Baghdad, but the almost-comedic hostilities raging between FOX News and MSNBC over which network's name-brand battlefield correspondent – and by extension, which network – was allegedly "more" patriotic and ethical. (Personally, I'd ignore them both – but must admit being very much in "shock and awe" observing the amusing efforts these two networks spent battling over this non-news issue.)

In addition, it was rare to see the American flag on a cable news channel until September 11, 2001. Now, almost two years later, computer-generated flags and other hints of Americana and supposed patriotism are a now-permanent fixture on cable news channels and their personalities as a constant reminder to viewers that America is "at war" — they should also serve as an indication of the channel's slant to presenting the news. It's hard to be objective when you're throwing one party's flag and national colors in the face of your viewers all the time, don't you think?

By comparison, the British Broadcasting Company (BBC) might be a state-operated media service, but its news organization's objectivity in both content and presentation format is without equal when compared to the corporate-controlled media services in the United States. (I prefer its news coverage to nearly anything produced in America.)

Suffice it to say, I don't have much faith in America's major news organizations' ability to inform and educate the public. If they spent as much time critically researching the day's events by asking the really tough questions that need to be answered that they do trying to win our trust as viewers through catchy phrases and clever on-air promotions, they wouldn't need to work so hard to earn it in the first place.

But it's not limited to just news organizations. Remember the uproar over comedian Bill Maher's comment that cowardice was demonstrated more by the risk-averse Clinton administration's repeated drive-by-shootings with cruise missiles against overseas terrorist camps than by the martyr-seeking suicide bombers of September 11th — and the Bush administration's response? After this incident started to make headlines, Maher's popular late-night show *Politically Incorrect* was cancelled, and he was made a whipping-boy by the administration simply for discussing something that ran contrary to the nation's Star-Spangled cognitive dissonance following September 11.

Despite any number of military officers and analysts who will agree that President Clinton's response to terrorism wasn't effective and didn't meet the problem head-on, Press Secretary Ari Fleischer's official response to the Maher quote was that "there are reminders to all Americans that they need to watch what they say, watch what they do, and this [post-September 11] is not a time for remarks like that; there never is."[13]

An even better example of the new American patriotic-or-else policy came from Attorney General John Ashcroft when he addressed the Senate Judiciary Committee in December 2001 on the Justice Department's efforts supporting the "war" on terror:

> To those who scare peace-loving people with phantoms of lost liberty, my message is this: Your tactics only aid terrorists for they erode our national unity and diminish our resolve. They give ammunition to America's enemies and pause to America's friends. They encourage people of good will to remain silent in the face of evil.[14]

Certainly, it's a necessity to have public support for military action, but — especially in a democratic society — not at the expense of the open discussion of the issues, including views or facts that may run contrary to the intended plans of action being proposed by the government. Yet as seen since September 11, the Administration is trying to ensure the American public is *always* and *unequivocally* supportive of its policies by implying that anything other would be unpatriotic — especially after making "you're either with us or with the terrorists" a declared national policy.

Or, to put it another way, as a prominent national leader in Europe noted while reflecting on his experiences during World War II,

> It is the leaders of the country who determine the policy and it is always a simple matter to drag the people along, whether it is a democracy, or a fascist dictatorship, or a parliament, or a communist

dictatorship. Voice or no voice, the people can always be brought to the bidding of the leaders. That is easy. All you have to do is tell them they are being attacked, and denounce the peacemakers for lack of patriotism and exposing the country to danger. It works the same in any country.

(This was said by Reichsmarschall Hermann Goering, the successor to Adolph Hitler as leader of Nazi Germany.)

Feeling opposed to new laws or policies that you don't agree with — or digging for too many detailed facts as a journalist or concerned citizen — suddenly made you seem anti-American, prone to harassment or arrest[15] and not simply a loyal, law-abiding dissenter with an alternative perspective on things. In one way or other, since September 11, citizens have been asked to sit down, shut up, spy on their friends and family, and to "be ready" (for another attack) yet "live normally" while continuing their unwavering support of their government as it folds, shreds, and mutilates their cherished Constitution in the name of "Homeland Security" — a disturbing trend that's discussed later on in this book.

And if you're a popular musician, or on-air personality at a media company – such as Clear Channel Communications – you had better be one-hundred-percent in-favor of the President or risk being fired or – in the case of the Dixie Chicks - not getting your songs played on their network of stations. Dissenting opinions – while a legal right for American citizens to express — are contrary to the popular good (and profits) in the eyes of America's ever-shrinking media industry, especially in an age where many such entities often masquerade as Republican propaganda machines.

It seems that Goering's spirit moved from Berlin and took up residence in Washington, D.C. but few people really took historical notice — choosing instead to go along with this way of thinking because they assume they're helping, they don't know any better, or they just don't care. So, just as with so many other national trends and cultural fads, like sheep, the American public moves whatever way they are herded toward by sound bytes, slogans, and carefully-contrived groupthink.

Think about it - does placing an American flag on your vehicle or lapel automatically make you a better American? Please. Try volunteering and giving something of yourself that makes a positive difference for others in need.

But this false sense of patriotism runs rampant in America. For example, a March 2002 editorial in the *Daytona Beach News-Journal* noted

> The nation's loyalty [for the War on Terror] is turning into groupthink.... What else can explain a president who, playing on the war's most visceral slogan, gets away with justifying an obscene corporate tax cut as 'economic security,' a build-up of defense industry stock as 'homeland security,' and an exploitative assault on the nation's most pristine lands as 'energy security'? What else explains his contempt for Congress, his Nixonian fixation on secrecy, his administration's junta-like demeanor in Washington since September 2001?[16]

At press time, the White House Web site indeed shows this trifecta[17] of security — national, economic, and homeland — as the three major policy items in the Bush administration.[18] Seems that since September 2001, anything with the word "security" in it sounds patriotic and destined to receive strong support despite whatever programs and initiatives are contained underneath.

The editorial concluded that it's not patriotism that keeps this runaway phenomenon rolling along; it's *the stupor of the American people.* As long as they're employed, have the basics of life, receive five hundred cable channels, own two SUVs, drink their beer, and live happily ever after, why should they care about such things? After all, *the real reason Americans elect leaders is so they don't have to think or worry* about that stuff. In a country famed for its creation of outsourcing as a way of corporate life, it really should surprise no one that Americans have groupthought[19] their way to outsourcing their need to think for themselves, and subsequently, relinquished personal control of their lives and ability to make a real difference in their nation.

When less than half of eligible voters in a society make the effort to vote, that society isn't a democracy, it's an oligarchy. And that's what America's turning out to be in 2003, despite patriotic claims to the contrary. Further, given the corrupt machine that is modern American politics, fewer and fewer people are willing to try to win elected public office; they know the odds are against them should they try and act on their conscience and challenge the status quo. Thus, American democracy continues on special-interest autopilot and — as some argue — is beginning to enter the proverbial death-spiral.

By their actions — but mainly through their inactions and ignorance — the American people are making themselves irrelevant in American society and governance. As a result, the democratic system America purportedly cherishes is rapidly giving way to the plutocratic interests of selected corporate entities and other special niche desires.

That's not just sad, it's shameful. About as shameful as laughing at our own ignorance on late-night television — especially for an information-based nation that prides itself as the "Beacon of Democratic Principles" for the world.

3

Spinning The Body Politic

You should say what you mean.
- The March Hare, in *Alice in Wonderland*

Almost all Washington insiders know that each word, phrase, and speech made by a political official is prepared carefully and well in advance of its delivery to ensure its language says only what is intended to be said and avoids creating an opportunity for misunderstanding or political exploitation by the opposite party. Generally, this is accomplished by what's known in White House press circles as the "message of the day" — or key words, phrases, and ideals that are woven into any public statements made during that time, often including colorful backgrounds with thematic messages such as "Creating More Jobs for America," or "Defending The Homeland."

Perhaps the American public would be able to understand America's political reality if they could pierce through the strategic word-smithing and on-screen artistry that taints nearly every public statement or media event regarding major policy issues.[20]

Given that this book is about seeing the reality of — and taking appropriate steps to improve — America's socio-political awareness, it's only appropriate to include a chapter on translating what is presented to the public by our media and elected officials so that readers can begin to sort through the political posturing and understand what is really being said — or not being said:

America's 2003 Political Lexicon: What They *Really* Mean To Say

Accountability: A term that implies holding someone responsible for their actions or inactions. Reality shows a different meaning, namely, to see who can avoid blame and still look good when bad things happen and ordinary people get hurt.

Affirmative Action: A federal program and philosophy once designed to ensure equal opportunity for Americans of *all* creeds, colors, and backgrounds but, over time, it has been converted into a form of reverse discrimination that's favorable to anyone except Caucasians. However, this shift is never challenged in politics because of the belief that anything called "affirmative" must be good for everyone involved, or else it wouldn't be called "affirmative" — and the fear that anyone challenging this program would be branded as racist.

Aggressive Driving: A politically correct term intended to describe actions taken by drivers who allegedly endanger others on the road. The term now has been perverted by local governments to embrace other common traffic violations such as failing to signal before changing lanes or simply speeding (but not in a reckless manner.) Being cited for aggressive driving affects drivers' records (and pocketbooks) more than being cited for traditional violations such as speeding, and also contributes to a municipality's annual revenue.

American People: Term used by politicians to imply who are the beneficiaries of their policies. In reality, the term is used to ensure that anyone challenging these policies — often benefiting only certain groups — will be seen as not looking out for the American public's best interests.

Analyst: Any semi-knowledgeable person who can express the well-founded opinion that most promotes his future career in the media; commonly seen as "Military Analyst" or "Political Analyst" during television interviews.

Animal Rights: A complimentary term used by both parties to persuade vegetarians to vote.

At-Risk: Paper-based category of people — generally children — who can be used as justification for an influx of federal dollars for ineffective social programs.

Background Source: An off-the-record term used to describe senior government officials who leak information to the press anonymously. When such leaks support an administration, they're tolerated; when they challenge an administration, they're dismissed as rumor and speculation.

Bipartisan: A term used by politicians referring to the cherished values of the democratic system and the "spirit of compromise." When used by the majority party to describe the successful passing of controversial legislation, it's a polite way of saying "the other side gave in and/or was out-voted." (See "Partisan")

Children: A last-ditch justification used for social programs, claiming that America's children will be endangered if the given policy item (e.g., gun control) passes or fails.

Committed: 1) A way for politicians to say they will deal with public issues without providing any specific details of their plans that could endanger their political standing. (E.g., "I'm committed to an America where every American has access to quality and affordable health care." How? Details, please!) 2)

The past tense of the verb describing what we should do with most of our politicians and narrow-minded pundits.

Community Outreach: Efforts by both major political parties to interact with the average person-on-the-street, often coming in the form of encouraging (or suppressing) one party's political agenda during campaign season.

Compassionate Conservatism: Process used to mask a certain political party's attempt to introduce closer links between organized religions (namely the Religious Right) and the policies of the American government.

Conservative: Once widely understood as one who adheres to traditional methods or views, Republicans now use this word to cover a broad range of social agendas such as: the consolidation of wealth in the hands of a few; intolerance of all religious traditions except certain sects of Christianity; and military budgets driven by the defense industry instead of actual threats to the nation.

Conservative Media: Epithet used by Democrats to discredit professional journalists who, as a result of their educational background, tend to be less narrow-minded than the average parochial politician and openly ask the questions nobody in government wants answered.

Constitutional Rights: Once the cornerstone of American law and a guaranteed feature of being an American citizen. Considered nowadays to be a series of flexible guidelines that can be sidestepped at will, provided it's sold to the public as necessary for "protecting" them; likely referred to by some in the Justice Department today as "Constitutional Privileges."

Corporate Reform: Efforts by politicians to clean up after corporate scandals but only if their own improprieties can be kept from public view while still ensuring adequate corporate contributions to their re-election campaigns.

Czar: Informal term for a Presidential appointee to coordinate the administration's programs on a given issue item. Such appointees — despite such a powerful-sounding moniker — have little real power and simply serve as glorified coordinators of such programs.

Democracy: A now-theoretical form of government that demands participation of a well-informed citizenry and encourages open, public debate. It is supposed to be administered by politicians of the highest integrity, something generally absent in modern American politics.

Deregulation: Formerly meant clearing away legal and other government obstacles to help establish a competitive marketplace; now used to mean the transition from *de jure* legal impediments to competition to *de facto* impediments such as unregulated and uncontrolled corporations or industries that are dictated by markets, not legislation.

Elections: Recurring process that determines which of the better of two bribed candidates (the lesser of two evils) is best qualified to support corporate interests and test the fiscal endurance of the American taxpayer. Also the only time when the average American citizen is conned into feeling they are an important and vital part of the American political process.

Employers: A more compassionate — and less corrupt-sounding — term for "business" used by politicians when addressing audiences comprised of America's working class. The implication is that "employers" provide (e.g., giving) much-needed jobs for workers while "business" is interested more in profits (e.g., taking) than its workers.

Employees: Term used by politicians when addressing corporate interest groups that refers to those on corporate payrolls who aren't executives. See also Workers.

End of Major Combat Operations: Newly-coined term that, loosely translated, means "We can't declare that a given 'war' is over, because all those we've captured so far in the conflict would have to be released according to international law, and we're just not ready to do that yet." In other words, a way to declare victory without actually declaring victory.

Fair and Balanced: Republican term referring to any arch-conservative news source serving as a tool of corporate (and Republican Party) interests while masquerading as an impartial public resource.

Fair: Implies justice, objectivity, and equal treatment by and for all concerned parties, but in reality refers to the special-interest needs of those who successfully lobbied for whatever is being described as "fair."

Faith-based: 1) A marketing euphemism for "religious-based" used as part of an attempt to circumvent the long-standing tenet of American law — the Bill of Rights — whose first ten words read "Congress shall make no law respecting an establishment of religion..." 2) Also a way to give government funds to certain religious groups who support the party in power.

Family values: A political euphemism used by conservative Republicans to appease its Religious Right supporters and justify homophobia, bigotry, and various other forms of intolerance and fear in society. Used to imply that anything other than a heterosexual relationship cannot be viewed as a "family" union.

First Amendment Zone: An officially-sanctioned place at political events where protesters can gather and make their cases known. Of course, such zones are so far removed from the main event, protesters are guaranteed very little mainstream press coverage for their causes, something that suits the majority just fine.

Flag: Since September 11, a necessary item to wave or display at all times and on all vehicles to avoid suspicion of being unpatriotic or supporting terrorism.

Free speech: Originally referring to the right of the people in a democracy to express and listen to the widest possible range of opinions in public. Also a rapidly disappearing concept given the consolidation of America's media outlets into a handful of entities uncomfortable with truly facilitating "free speech" by promoting diverse or contrary positions regarding the issues of the day.

Friday Quiet Time: Any time late on a Friday afternoon when government entities like to release less-than-stellar (or small but embarrassing) news items to the public, knowing that by the time Monday arrives, the bad news will be overtaken by better news on a different topic, especially if journalists eager to go home don't get the story beforehand.

Gun Control: Efforts to confiscate personal guns and repeal the Second Amendment under the mistaken belief that a gun — an inanimate object — can kill people by itself.

Gun Safety: See "Gun Control."

Homeland: A patriotic term referring to a geographic area occupied by people under a common government to inculcate a sense of pride and support for the government's policies to protect it. Traditionally associated with the closed police-state societies under Soviet communism during the Cold War, known then as the Motherland. See also "Homeland Security."

Homeland Security: A historically-blind justification for politicians to shred America's Constitution, expand government bureaucracy, and create thousands of new federal jobs by perpetuating the belief that the dangers of international terrorism requires such changes to be implemented without question or meaningful public debate. See also "Homeland."

Illiteracy: Inability to write or read simple texts; a condition caused by inferior education systems, listening to cliché-ranting politicians, playing too many video games, or watching too much mindless commercial television.

Incursion: Modern expression replacing the more accurate term "attack" when performed by the United States (or any other friendly state) against an opponent deemed unfriendly to the United States.

Independent Media: Journalists and pundits not associated with commercial news organizations who uncover questionable issues and bring them to the public attention. Often times these entities are dismissed by policymakers and mainstream media organizations because they're not toeing the accepted party line and can't be influenced by political or corporate pressures. In rare cases, independent media sources break a major story that is picked up by the mainstream news sources and thus serve as a *de facto* media watchdog.

Internet: A vast medium of free expression and new ideas that will eventually require silencing, as it's the untamed evil that corrupts the minds of American children (see "children"), fosters the alleged theft of vast quantities of copyrighted material, and potentially supports terrorism.

Journalism: A profession in which practitioners are supposed to inform the general public of the true state of affairs in society, but which lately has deteriorated (with few admirable exceptions) to those who simply tell the public what government officials want them to be told while keeping themselves employed and publicly-popular by suppressing uncomfortable truths from readers and viewers.

Less Government: Euphemism for policies giving big corporations and wealthy individuals license to employ unscrupulous business practices, produce dangerous products, pollute the air and water, and monopolize the market by allowing business lobbying groups to write the laws governing their regulation. A practice similar to the proverbial fox guarding the proverbial henhouse.

Liberal: Once commonly used to mean "one who is open minded," Republicans have successfully redefined this word to mean anyone not totally supportive of their policies, programs, and leadership. Accusing anyone in Washington of being a "liberal" is akin to accusing someone of having "cooties" in elementary school.

Liberal Media: Epithet used by Republicans to discredit professional journalists who, as a result of their educational background, tend to be less narrow-minded than the average parochial politician and openly ask the questions that nobody in government wants answered.

Lies: Almost everything spoken publicly by political and corporate leaders as they attempt to portray facts or the "truth" to suit their political agenda.

Loyal Dissent: The patriotic act of legally expressing one's views to the public to promote social or political policy changes even though such views may be contrary to the status quo. Something most ruling majorities must by law tolerate but tend to make as irrelevant as it can to avoid answering embarrassing questions.

Mom-and-Pop: A softer term used in public speeches to conjure up rosy images of traditional American households — think of the *"Brady Bunch"* or *"Leave It To Beaver"* — and imply that anything else isn't a caring, American "family" entity. See also "Family values."

National Interest: 1) Legitimate policy goal to pursue if done within internationally agreed frameworks and agreements. 2) Illegitimate policy goal to pursue by intervention, intimidation, bombing, destabilization, blackmail, coercion or other means frowned upon by the international community.

National Security: 1) Frequently used justification to conceal from public scrutiny embarrassing papers concerning political stupidity, mistakes and criminal activity. 2) Invoked to avoid answering tough questions about any national policy, particularly after September 11.

Nationalization: The government-funded solution to everything, often creating thousands of new jobs and expanded federal government bureaucracy such as the Department of Homeland Security; but in reality accomplishes little, if anything, effectively.

Partisan: Used to describe any mean-spirited, illegitimate, and/or allegedly-unpatriotic attempt by the minority political party to question, challenge, or publicly debate the majority party's vaunted "nonpartisan" policies. See also: "Bi-Partisan."

Patriot: 1) Anyone believing in the infallibility of American policy as proposed by the Administration and will accept on blind faith whatever they're asked to without question, particularly in a time of national emergency.   See also: "Traitor." 2) Anyone caring deeply for their nation's well-being and desires a better future for his fellow citizen, but not at the expense of the core values that their nation was founded on. See also: "Loyal Dissent."

Patriotism: Invoked by politicians to ensure unquestioning loyalty from the masses when doing questionable things often detrimental to their best interest and well-being.

Patriot Act: 1) A massive law passed within two months of its introduction in Congress — a speed rarely seen in Washington — following September 11; it provides sweeping new privacy invasions and surveillance of Americans by police in an effort to "prevent" future terrorism. 2) A legal document that proves that you can get away with anything as long as you call it patriotic and wrap it in the American flag.

Person of Interest: An individual that, in the eyes of federal law enforcement (or political spin-meisters,) exhibits signs that they may be an unpatriotic American and thus a potential terrorist. Such activities include the legal exercise of their rights, thinking for themselves, or voting other than Republican. See also: "Loyal Dissent."

Politics: Term used to disparage opponents on a given issue - a catch-all term that implies no matter what the other party is saying, or how right their facts may be, they're only saying such things to win my elected seat next year. (It's sort of like how kids explain their actions in that infamous term "because.")

Political Action Committee (PAC): Lobbying organizations on Capitol Hill, also known as those who ask their elected officials to Please Accept Cash (it's harder to trace.) See "Special interests."

Preempt: Doing something unto somebody else before he can do it unto you, regardless of whether he has any plans or means to do it. If your allies disagree with you, it's not your problem — it's your self-claimed right as the stronger party.

Pro-Choice: Those who believe that when it comes to sexual health, the control of women's bodies should be governed by the individual woman involved and not the dogma of certain religious organizations.

Pro-Life: Those who believe that when it comes to sexual health, the control of women's bodies should be governed by the dogma of certain religious organizations and not the woman involved.

Public school: Publicly-funded buildings where children learn to recognize corporate logos and (in the vast majority of cases) become indoctrinated as the functional, task-oriented drones of tomorrow's society.

Religious Right: People in the many groups comprising this segment of America's voters tend to justify homophobia, bigotry, and various other forms of intolerance as they strive to morally-cleanse America's diverse social values and replace them with a bible-thumping, Christian, God-fearing one.

Revisionist: 1) A derogatory term referring to anyone offering a public perspective that's different from the President's view on the world. See also: "Loyal Dissent." 2) A President who spins half-truths and speculation as fact to fit his international policy agenda.

Sound byte: A portion of a political speech that becomes a *de facto* policy statement due to its popularity and frequent use despite the reality of the issue being discussed (e.g., "axis of evil" and "you're either with us or with the terrorists"). In other words, a short phrase that won't strain the intellectual capacity of the average American.

Special interests: Any entity or organization exchanging their influence, money, or resources for the unwavering support of government officials on policy items of interest to them or their members See "Political Action Committee."

Staffers: While elected officials get the public attention and make the speeches, it's the unseen legions of highly stressed, poorly paid staff members in Congress, the White House, and elsewhere that actually develop policies and laws before presenting them to their bosses for review and action. In addition to elected officials, certain key staffers also are courted by special interest groups when pressing their agendas and sometimes more important to know than the actual elected official they work for.

"Strong (or Very Good) Support:" When used in foreign policy circles, this phrase implies staunch support for American ventures overseas by key countries. In reality, it can mean anything from overly providing troops and basing rights to unseen economic support or quiet promises made behind the scenes with little or no public mention.

Sunday Funnies: Sunday morning news programs where invited government officials can present prepared talking points on the issue-of-the-week, and one of the few places on commercial television where a senior government official can spend an hour talking and say absolutely nothing.

Taxes: Government-mandated payments collected from the largest (and poorest) part of the population and used for the things that the smallest (and wealthiest) part wants.

Television: 1) An electronic device known to turn thinking individuals into moronic accepters of political and "entertainmental" stupidities. 2) The best brainwashing device ever invented for commercial or political use.

Town Hall Meeting: A televised gathering of local citizens who ask scripted or pre-screened questions to elected officials or candidates to present an image of American democracy in action.

Traitor: Term applied to non-Christian humanists who may be domestic enemies of the state (e.g., non-Republicans,) foreign enemies (e.g., Communists,) or those who continuously exercise their common sense and legal rights by politely and legally questioning the legitimacy of the their government's seemingly runaway policies.

Truth: Whatever information or knowledge a person or organization cares to present to (or not withhold from) the public or investigators. In the case of Iraq's weapons program, the President says we will find "the truth" – even if it shows there *wasn't* a program of the magnitude presented to the public in the run-up to the war. (The "truth" is a very subjective thing, especially in politics and the media.)

Two-Party System: The misguided belief perpetuated by both Democrats and Republicans that a third political party is two more than America really needs.

Unilateralism: Inability or unwillingness to cooperate with other counties unless they do exactly what America expects them to do. The opposite, so-called 'multilateralism,' can be achieved either through reasonable compromises with all involved or by threats and bribes in the case when one party is equipped with enough weapons and stupidity.

War: 1) Committing military forces intending to battle and successfully overcome the enemy. 2) A marketing term used by politicians to describe (and seek public praise for) committing federal resources to combat a social problem such as drugs, AIDS, or poverty, regardless of how successful it is.

Weapons of Mass Destruction: Large quantities of some really bad weapons that the US government thought it necessary to go to war in Iraq to eliminate, yet three months after the "end of major combat operations" has yet to discover.

Weapons of Mass Delusion: Things the American people and government think are associated with freedom and cherished American values – things that, in reality, often are quite ugly and run contrary to such values. The topic of this book, actually.

Weapons of Mass Distraction: Anything used to divert the media and gullible public's attention from facts that could cause political embarrassment, such as why America hasn't found any weapons of mass destruction in Iraq yet (you mean the primary goal of war *wasn't* to "liberate the Iraqi people?") or the Bush administration's close ties with Enron and the California energy crisis.

Workers: Term used by politicians when addressing working-class groups that refers to those on corporate payrolls who aren't executives. See also Employees.

4

Why Stop The Buck, When You Can Pass It?

Computer games don't affect kids; I mean, if Pac-Man affected us as kids, we'd all be running around in darkened rooms, munching magic pills and listening to repetitive electronic music.
- Kristian Wilson, Nintendo, Inc, 1989

With every new shooting in America — whether a school shooting, a worker gone postal, or the Washington, D.C. "Beltway Snipers" of 2002 — pundits and so-called "family values" groups assemble to reassert their belief in the need to restrict or eliminate the sale of video games,[21] music,[22] or movies[23] deemed violent or offensive. And let's not forget about getting rid of all those nasty guns while we're at it. Guns are evil, right?

Obviously, it's the music and video games that make an individual trip over the edge into murderous rage, and not mental illness, sociopathic tendencies, bad parenting, or any combination of the above. Common sense would dictate that just because an Eminem CD was found in the stereo doesn't mean the song lyrics drove its owner to kill someone. But, unfortunately, it seems common sense is in short supply in America these days.

While a rational person understands that guns don't kill people by themselves — a person must point the inanimate object at someone and pull the trigger — according to gun-control advocacy groups the gun makers are at fault, since they manufactured the weapon involved. Of course, not to be outdone, "family values" groups can be equally vocal in blaming the video game makers, musicians, and anyone else they deem anti-*"family values"* for the tragedy.

Like many of our current politicians and government officials, these advocacy groups are content to treat a symptom of society's ills rather then the disease itself. You see, traditionally, Americans tend to hurt themselves and then look around to find out whose fault it was.

Take children, for instance. The war cry of "for the children" sends shivers down the backs of many — especially video game makers, movie studios, and record companies — who learned the hard and costly way that you don't want to tangle with these advocacy groups.

But rather than take this power and create a platform encouraging parental responsibility, these groups manage to place blame every-and-anywhere but with the parents. It's *never* the parents' fault if a child goes on a school-shooting spree — it's the music. A child is violent? — must be the video games or movies. A child does drugs, steals, or drives drunk? Blame it on the movie or liquor companies. If a child commits suicide, blame can be heaped on the Internet and Black Sabbath lyrics — anywhere but where it should be placed to really fix the situation.

Apparently, personal responsibility in 2003 only goes so far — especially if being responsible becomes embarrassing or too tough to handle. People would much rather point fingers and sue anyone and everyone instead of facing and dealing with their own stupidity, carelessness, or complacency. So they try to sue their way to becoming a more responsible (or self-assured) person under the rubric of being a "victim" in any number of goofy, frivolous lawsuits. Passing the buck has become the New American Way.

In recent years, frivolous lawsuits come in second only to the infamous annual "Darwin Award" for demonstrating collective human idiocy. It's also a booming new American industry. After all, if there's money to be made that requires little or no effort, people will find a way to get their share of the pie, especially in today's hard economic times. Besides, what's a little humiliation on the path to free riches?

Some of these entrepreneurs — some of them successful — include:

- Michael Croteau, who in 2002 brought a $300,000 lawsuit against his local hockey association because his son — with the highest number of goals that season and a distinguished playing record in previous years — wasn't awarded the league's Most Valuable Player award or named to Canada's Winter Games team.[24] The rationale here seems to be that if someone doesn't win something that they or their parents' think they should, a lawsuit is an acceptable way to turn their frown upside down. Yet, any good coach will tell you that the MVP title isn't based exclusively on performance, but teamwork, attitude, sportsmanship, and any number of other off-field qualities. Talk about suing your way to victory!

- Michele Nations, who in 1994 received a $450,000 award against the city of Tucson, Arizona because she tripped over a gopher hole in a city-owned park.[25] Apparently, Americans are no longer responsible for looking where they are going when walking. Would she have sued herself if she'd tripped over a coffee table at home?

- An Idaho college student who in 1994 sued the college for not providing warnings about the dangers of upper-story windows after he fell from his third-floor window while "mooning" his classmates.[26]

- In 2000, McDonalds was sued because a man who purchased a milkshake from the drive-up window spilled the frosty beverage in his lap, which caused him to collide with another car. The clumsy driver believed Mickey-D's should warn customers about the dangers of eating and driving.[27]

- In Tampa, Florida, Ed O'Rourke sued the local power company and a host of Tampa bars after a 1996 incident when he was shocked with over 13,000 volts of electricity breaking into a secured utility substation and climbing up on a power transformer while drunk.[28] He claimed that local bars continued serving him alcohol even though he was "unable to control his urge to drink alcoholic beverages."

- In 1999, the parents of a twenty-seven year old man sued Sea World Orlando when their adult-aged son was found naked and dead after jumping into the 50-degree water tank housing the park's Orca whales.[29] The parents said the park was negligent by portraying the Orca's as safe and huggable creatures in their marketing brochures.

- A man sued beer manufacturer Anheuser-Busch for $10,000 claiming false advertising.[30] He alleged that he suffered mental and physical injury from the implied promises of the beer maker's advertisements; when he drank large amounts of their brand of beer, he didn't have success meeting women, and also ended up getting sick. He apparently overlooked the benefits his beer provided in helping his body "flush itself out" later that night.

- A devout Hindu man sued Taco Bell for serving him a meat burrito instead of a vegetarian one, seeking significant compensation for the emotional distress and financial losses required to religiously purify his body after this transgression.[31] Of course, he could never admit to looking at his meal before taking that first juicy, beefy bite ... that would have been the normal and safe thing to do, especially at a Taco Bell.

- In late 2002, Caesar Barber, 56, a New York City maintenance worker suffering from obesity, two heart attacks, and diabetes, sued several American fast-food restaurants, claiming they didn't warn him that frequently eating large meals at their locations each week might endanger his health.[32]

That last one has got to be the icing on the cake for frivolous and stupid lawsuits brought by ignorant and irresponsible people. But then again, this is happening in the nation where eating a thousand-calorie lunch - but insisting on having a Diet Cola with it to "avoid the calories" - is the norm in society. Need I say more?

As John Doyle, co-founder of the Center for Consumer Freedom, pointed out about the Barber case, "to win his suit, he has to convince a jury or a judge that people are too stupid to feed themselves or their children. If people are so stupid, should they be allowed to vote or go to work in the morning?"[33]

It appears that the nation founded on principles of independence, self-reliance, and *Poor Richard's Almanac* has devolved into the nation where no one wants to be responsible for anything; a nation where being an idiot *can* make you rich, assuming you don't mind a little embarrassment or public scorn along the way and can find a group of citizens on a jury who are dumb enough to reward you for your own stupidity.

Remember this when requesting a jury trial by your peers.

5

Newsporn

What the mass media offers is not popular art, but entertainment which is intended to be consumed like food, forgotten, and replaced by a new dish.
- W. H. Auden, *The Dyer's Hand*

In today's twenty-four hour news environment, news programs (or what currently passes for news programs) no longer feel obligated to simply report the facts — or even reality.

Remember the frenzy over child abductions during the summer of 2002? From one kidnapping in California, the summer's media exploded with daily stories regarding child abductions and tips for child safety, and quickly generated a tidal wave of fear across America. All this hype and fear fueled public interest in the subject despite FBI and private-sector statistics clearly showing a significant decrease in the number of abductions during that time.[34] The same could be said about 2001's "Summer of the Shark" – an issue that was seriously overblown by the media as a public safety concern despite official statistics to the contrary.[35]

Clearly, the media exploits such issues to sow fear in America's family audiences and gain viewers and readers for its advertisers. That's to be expected, since thanks to the continuous cable news cycle, fewer advertiser dollars, and the fickle nature of the average television viewer, news networks must be able to keep eyeballs glued to their coverage — and from clicking away to the ever-shrinking competition. After all, news is first and foremost a business more interested in profits and attracting viewers than informing or challenging audiences to think for themselves.

This has managed to turn what was once hardcore news — meaning events and situations that the public *should* be concerned about — into a sensational multimedia circus that Barnum and Bailey would envy. Forget about learning *why* the day's events happen — the emphasis is to show them *as* they happen — instead of serious reports and analysis by educated anchors and reporters, we now have raw action, speculation, unconfirmed reports, and tearful interviews presented and accompanied by high-tech graphics, factoids popping up in easily digestible bullet-charts, logos, coming attractions, and never-ending news feeds scrolling across the bottom of the television screen, all with the ultimate goal of keeping viewers glued to the screen to see what happens next.

It's no different than watching pornography.

Like an alluring lesbian sex scene involving *"Naked College Cheerleaders"* on pay-per-view, television news viewers are brought along on an audiovisual trip that compels them to stay on the edge of their seats, desperate to find out what happens next and how things ultimately will turn out. Flashy graphics, music to "fit the mood" and experts from all walks of life are brought into newsrooms across America to help dispense what's become less news and more "info-tainment" programming for the masses.

If in doubt, just think about the around-the-clock television coverage of the first ten days of Operation IRAQI FREEDOM in 2003. Some might say this was the ultimate "reality television" programming venture, complete with "embedded reporters" and green-tinted night-vision cameras covering the action in near-real-time; viewers were quickly mesmerized by jerky video filmed while bouncing along Iraqi roads or ducking for cover while accompanying a combat unit under enemy fire

— they had never seen this type of footage before outside of the movies or computer games before. Would the camera show more action? Would the unit be under attack again? What was the maximum driving range of that Bradley Fighting Vehicle? Were those Marines carrying M-16 rifles or M-4 carbines? How many bullets – or "rounds" as we learned the military calls them — do they carry? What options did the military have for surrounding and capturing Baghdad, and what kind of resistance would the Iraqi Special Republican Guard put up against our troops? Stay tuned and find out!

And stay tuned, the viewers did.

Essentially, this was porn the whole family could watch - it was scripted action without substance, content without a higher context, and it appealed to our basic emotional instinct for raw, physical action. Definite porn-like characteristics. And in prime-time, too!

The networks love this kind of programming because it meant more eyeballs for their premium advertisers once they began running commercials after the war began. And viewers were kept on the sensory edge, constantly teased and continually wanting more, but never really feeling satisfied. So they stuck around to see what happens next, which meant watching through a few profitable commercial breaks without changing channels. (And in the case of "embedded journalists," the Pentagon loved it because they could keep tabs on many of the influential reporters in the field with American forces.)

That being said, there is big money to be made in the network and cable news industry, and I'd be foolish not to try and get a piece of the pie myself. So in an effort to offer my services to the industry, here are some examples of my ideas on the off chance someone would like to consider offering me a lectern to teach news production — or better yet — run a news station:

HOW TO PRODUCE NEWS LIKE THE PROS

1. Develop a catchy name to describe the news story, such as "Summer of the Shark," "Showdown With Saddam," or "Terror in The Classroom" that can be emblazoned across the screen for the duration of your coverage. Even if you're currently airing a financial news program, such logos can draw channel-surfers to your network.

2. Use as many close-up images from helicopters circling over the scene as you can get (without crashing into any other news helicopters, that is.) This will provide viewers with a sense of drama and a vantage point not normally seen by everyday people. This format works regardless if you're covering a school shooting, schools of sharks, a plane crash, or a white Bronco creeping down a Los Angeles freeway.

3. Ensure that all press conferences related to the story are labeled "Breaking News" or the "Latest Development" and interrupt all but the most valuable prime time programming to bring it to your viewers live. Remember to preview what "Latest Development" will be covered when you resume programming after commercials to keep your viewers watching through the commercial break.

4. Record and broadcast comments and observations about the event from friends, relatives, classmates, co-workers, church-mates, and anyone else that can pronounce the name of the killer/terrorist/victim/day of the week. This should include the local Avon Lady if she's available, especially if she knew someone involved and sold them something.

5. As for shootings, be sure to interview the people who hid from (or even heard) the gunfire. In the case of school shootings, close-ups of teenage girls hugging and consoling each other are essential. Despite the circumstances, dazed freshmen talking with guidance or grief counselors are golden opportunities made for television. Take advantage of those moments. Any shootings that are outside the profile of *regular* daily homicides in your city should be hyped as a major event, to include speculating about if it might be related to terrorism, the Loch Ness Monster, or the Lindbergh Baby kidnapping.

6. During any emergency, get plenty of extra footage of people fleeing the scene and victims on stretchers being rushed to ambulances. This can be used throughout the week for supplemental coverage as your anchors rehash it during lags in the story — such as when an uplink to an on-site reporter or expert fails — and goes far in developing interest and speculation for a prime-time special your channel will host later on the event. Remember, blood sells!

7. Have your design department develop graphics and maps showing the location of (or anything even remotely) related to the event. In the case of a shooting, indicate the routes people took to flee or evacuate the building, and the locations where each bullet was fired. If you're covering a plane crash, show the radius the plane could have flown (had it not crashed) with a full tank of gas, its interior floor plan, and what it looks like intact. Bonus points if the graphics are animated. If covering a military scoop, a background image of a rotating radar screen is always appropriate.

8. Provide a minute-by-minute account of the killer/ victim/ terrorist/ suspect's day, from when they woke until they were captured/ killed/ injured/ escaped. If you can find what the suspect had for breakfast, use it to lead the evening broadcast.

9. Find someone who can say they knew the event was going to happen before it did, learning about it from an Internet chat room, website, or witnessing suspicious behavior exhibited by the perpetrator. In rare cases, carefully controlled speculation supported by leading questions is acceptable, especially in the first few hours after an event. If you can get a screen shot of any Internet chat room material, or a close up of notes, poems, receipts or any other item people found odd, you have at least a three-day supply of reusable on-air material. Make sure you have writing analysts, psychiatrists, therapists, and other specialists on-call to pore endlessly over the item(s) in question.

10. In cases where a non-Caucasian was killed or injured, interview local minority leaders to determine whether this tragedy was race-related.

11. During the first few hours of a tragedy, include interviews with respected psychologists — scratchy cell phones make for a more dramatic presentation — discussing how and why such events occur, what motivates the perpetrators, and offering guidance for the victims on how best to grieve.

12. Bring a respected security or law enforcement consultant into your studio to provide ongoing analysis about the event. In the case of school shootings, they should discuss the viability and need for cameras, metal detectors, and photo identification in schools. If the issue is terrorism, the experts could discuss the various types of gas masks and remind viewers that although such an item won't protect them much, it's still "a good thing" to have at home.

13. Develop appropriate theme music for your coverage. It should either be ominous and sinister (suggesting impending doom) or muted but fast-paced, such as how viewers perceive how newsrooms operate. Good networks have this stuff stockpiled and ready to go.

14. For major gun-related stories, host a studio debate that includes gun control advocates using the tragedy as proof that

America needs stronger gun laws. This should be balanced with a spokesman from the regional NRA chapter insisting that existing gun laws are fine, and that further gun control laws will not help keep guns away from criminals. The public never tires of a good gun-control debate.

15. For school-shooting stories, develop a special-interest feature for the late evening news on how to recognize the signs that your teenager may become a homicidal maniac. Be sure to include the critical signs like an interest in staying out late with friends, becoming distant from family members, and wearing black clothing.

16. Be sure to develop and announce online surveys for viewers to participate in via the Internet. Questions like "Are gun control laws in America strong enough?" or "How likely do you think another shooting will take place in your town?" are great ways to get large numbers of votes by people dumb enough to put down their dinners and rush into the living room to log on and cast their votes. On the off chance that not many people participate, you can always fake the results — these aren't scientific polls, and besides, who's going to know?

17. Pay any amount of money to steal Geraldo "Combat Reporter" Rivera away from whatever network he's currently shilling for. Although he's overly sensational, people seem to like him, which means more middle-class viewers for your advertisers to drool over.

NOTES TO THE CLASS:

Always remember that the longer you can keep the words **"BREAKING NEWS"** on the screen, the longer people will stay tuned in, and more channel surfers will stop to watch your coverage, even if nothing "breaking" is happening and you're many hours into covering the event.

If you can get good theme music to play when the "BREAKING NEWS" logo comes on, it will call out to the audience and draw them back into the room if they have wandered off. Eventually, in a time-tested Pavlovian reaction, your audience will be drawn to the TV whenever that music plays and those eyeballs will be yours for a good long time.

And remember, even if you don't have much "news" in your presentation, that's okay. After all, it's only info-tainment – and besides, this is America.

6

Regarding Political Correctness In Schools

In the first place God made idiots. This was for practice. Then he made school boards.
 - Mark Twain

The 'memorandum' shown below was intended to serve as a satirical parody of the politically-correct state of America's public school system.

Little did I know that the teachers – from public and private schools and colleges — who saw this memo in its early stages would offer their own guidance in 'drafting' it based on their own experiences in their respective schools. In this case, I almost wish literature didn't reflect reality quite so well.

In reviewing this chapter, they all wondered what our overly-politicized, special-interest-influenced, corporate-subsidized public education system is coming to, and what that means for the future of America's adult society.

So did I.

WEAPONS OF MASS DELUSION

MEMORANDUM TO: All School Principals
SUBJECT: Curriculum Revisions
FROM: I. M. Dopey,
                 Superintendent, Local School Board
DATE: Sometime Soon

Welcome to the New School Year! I hope everyone had a great summer.

As educators we must remember that our first priority is to our students. After last month's Board Meeting — when a group of concerned parents raised valid points regarding questionable (or unfair) academic programs and social issues offensive to their respective beliefs — we realized that as educators we've been found deficient in several areas and must take decisive steps guaranteeing that all our students will be able to learn in a safe, non-offensive, non-repressive environment.

In direct response to the issues raised, please be advised that our district will move quickly to address each specific concern regarding any academic or social program deemed offensive, intrusive, sexist, racist, or in any way belittling to students' self esteem. Additionally, please note that these guidelines will be drafted into a formal policy statement by our next Board Meeting.

Until then, this guidance memorandum shall be received and acted upon as an official policy statement:

- Boys shall not stare at girls, and vice-versa. Such activities are inappropriate and may be offensive to those students with a proclivity toward same-sex relationships. These students deserve equal tolerance and respect in our district.

- All sports and related competitive activities (to include spelling and math competitions) must be discontinued immediately. Competition of any sort is simply too devastating to a child's self-esteem, especially when that child fails to win his or her event. By removing the potential for a child to lose, they will remain cheerful and confidently continue meeting the challenges of daily school life.

- While our student athletes are free to practice by themselves or as a team to become better players, they are prohibited from competing against other schools. Additionally, the practice of "Shirts and Skins" to identify teams is prohibited, as it may be seen as separating people based on their external appearances.

- As seen in Connecticut[36] and elsewhere, we also will establish a District Bullying Task Force to explore ways of eliminating cliques in the student body that lead to ridicule, "you-can't-play-on-my-team" comments, and other nastiness that might offend another student's self-esteem. This includes ensuring that no student is left off the invitation list for a classmate's birthday party. We must continue to foster a caring, egalitarian, social environment for our students, both inside the classroom and out.

- To eliminate the elitist stigma associated with evaluating academic performance in our the traditional lettered grading system, the "Pass/Fail" grading system will be introduced this year to reflect our new spirit of recognizing all our student's *efforts* in striving for excellence. We must recognize that each student has different capabilities for knowledge, and as educators we should not discriminate amongst them, or simply praise a select few students with above-average intellects. (Note: Only students routinely absent from academic instruction will be awarded a "Fail" mark, as they did not submit any work for review.)

- Art classes shall be eliminated, as it is unfair to those that are color blind or not good with modeling clay. Music classes will also be eliminated, as it is unfair to the tonally-challenged and hearing-impaired members of the student body. Likewise, choir is to be eliminated, as embarrassing situations might occur when a student's voice cracks.

- Social studies are far too controversial, as they cover topics like religion, war, slavery, alcohol and the oppression of women. These may be uncomfortable topics for our students, and we must do our best to avoid discussing them. Instead, educators should focus on promoting unwavering trust in our elected leaders, and reinforcing at all times that America is a democratic utopia of many different races, faiths, and people. Please remember, however, that we should not discuss how the Puritans or any other ethnic, racial, or religious group arrived — or survived — in this country as this might lead to the uncomfortable discussions mentioned above. (Note: Due to these changes, annual Thanksgiving and Christmas plays and celebrations shall be cancelled and instead "A Day of Multi-Culturalism Observance" will be celebrated across the district.)

- February will remain "Black History Month" but starting next year, we will also have "Asian Appreciation Month" in October and "White History Month" in December to provide equal opportunity for students to embrace and cherish these different cultures.

- Math classes and the various numbers or symbols may be too difficult for dyslexics to handle and so, effective immediately, we will remove them from our curriculum.

- Given the cultural diversity of our student population and the fact we cannot mandate the study of English to students whose first language isn't American English, all English classes will be replaced with "Language Arts" offering reading and writing instruction in English, Spanish, Arabic, and Ebonics, for starters.

- During the next year, we will modify our entire academic program to reflect the spirit of tolerance our district must demonstrate. This will entail avoiding using textbooks or pencils (both come from trees) or pens (made from plastics, a byproduct of petroleum). Further, to help stem the global waste of food, all Home Economics students will be required to consume whatever foods they prepare as classroom assignments, unless it offends them, in which case they may offer it to a classmate.

- Our libraries need major revisions. Visually-impaired children can only read Braille, and we cannot have printed, non-Braille books on the stacks. But since that would be an affront to the students who *can* see, we must eliminate the Braille books as well. Thus, everyone will be treated fairly, and there won't be any cause for controversy.

- The problems in the cafeteria will continue to plague us and anger parents until we address them. It has been deemed unfair that children of Jewish and Muslim faiths cannot eat the pepperoni pizzas, hamburgers, and hot dogs served for lunch. Vegetarian students may be offended at the sight of others eating cooked animal flesh or drinking milk and become upset at the district's flagrant disregard for cows' rights. In addition, we must consider removing all dairy products, fish, peanuts, sugar, and fruits, in respect for those with those food allergies. (After careful review of the required courses of action mentioned above, the district believes that students will eat better if they bring lunch from home. The district can then save on the expenses associated with running and staffing a cafeteria five days a week.

- Naptime will be removed from kindergartens, as those with sleep disorders (such as insomnia) may feel uncomfortable when they encounter those with bedwetting problems lying next to them.

- Students will be prohibited from listening to music on personal stereos or compact disk players, since their choice of music may be offensive to others if they've got their headset volume turned up too high or start singing along.

- Students should be encouraged to express themselves creatively in class projects; however, such creativity must be kept within the guidelines of this memorandum and not offend anyone or seem outside the norms of the guidance of this memorandum.

One final note: The School Board's preliminary ban on dodge ball is now permanent. It was determined that the game is too competitive and encourages aggression in an environment where the strong and clever pick on the weak, and the strongest or most clever student ultimately wins. How this game can "prepare children for life" without hurting their self-esteem is unknown, and thus it must not be played on school grounds or at school events.

We firmly believe these changes will make our school district a more appropriate place for students to learn, foster a sense of community and tolerance, and enable them to fully prepare to deal with the rigors of life.

See you in the teachers' lounge!

7

Schoolyard Stalag

Real education must ultimately be limited to men who insist on knowing. The rest is mere sheep-herding.
　　　　　　- Ezra Loomis Pound

The 1989 Robin Williams' film *Dead Poet's Society* had an interesting philosophy that we don't see much of any more: students should be allowed to think for themselves and be free to explore their own creativity.

For a brief, shining moment, it seemed as if this idea might take off, as pundits held this movie up not as an example of necessary education reform, but in reaction to the shootings that plagued mainly Midwestern schools during the 1990s. As a result, public schools across the country are now on-watch for trench coats, gothic appearances, quiet behaviors, angry demeanors, outsiders, students interested in horror novels, and creative writing that's less violent than Shakespeare's *Hamlet* — which is required reading in many high school literature classes. (And my parents thought a boy with a ponytail was a problem child.)

Now, after a skid-like ten year, 360-degree turn, students are not only discouraged from thinking for themselves, they can forget about any form of independent creative expression unless it conforms to school policies and overall political correctness.

We've seen students suspended or expelled from schools for doodling pictures of guns, submitting "scary" stories as creative writing assignments, carrying fingernail clippers, wearing black clothing or makeup, dying their hair, believing in alternative religions, or even using the word "shoot" in casual conversation. And woe unto the occasional student who — during a time of war — wears a shirt displaying a picture of the president with the caption "International Terrorist" on it to school; despite that quiet display of his sentiments toward national policy, he might be ordered to remove the shirt or go home for the day, since it might upset other, perhaps less-tolerant, members of the student body.[37]

Recently, the Blue Springs, Missouri police department submitted a grant request for over $250,000 to investigate what draws the youth of that town to the music, books, magazines, jewelry, fashion trends, movies, comic books, and other characteristics of Gothic culture that many teens gravitate toward during their angst-filled years.[38] The department noted in its request that it needed to get a handle on Gothic culture which emphasizes a deep morbidity — revealing itself in its adherents dressing in black, makeup (for girls *and* boys), dirge-like music and fascination with deeply disturbing poetry (Poe, Baudelaire, Dickinson) and writing (Stephen King, Clive Barker) and, most alarming, the fact that these maladjusts appear to hang out with like-minded folks — and this is just not *normal* adolescent behavior.

Goth culture therefore must be a breeding ground for potential troublemakers, along with violent video games, music, and ailments only treatable by prescription drugs.

The Texas Crime Prevention Center even classifies Goth-rock fans as "gangs" that likely engage in criminal activity, and suggests monitoring the library books borrowed and the Internet sites visited by these teens to identify these allegedly "at-risk" children.[39]

In general, it's knee-jerk thinking like this that, in recent years, is responsible for introducing identification cards, surveillance cameras, metal detectors, perimeter fencing, and psychological profiles for students to determine who *might* be a troublemaker in American public schools. The chilling concept of "Pre-Crime" depicted in the 2002 movie *"Minority Report"* may not be as far-fetched or far-off as it seemed.

In the case of our young, we're running around trying to pre-empt everything these days, but no matter how well intentioned, this has the unfortunate side effect of regarding anyone marginally outside the "acceptable norm" as a potential threat. And like the paranoia-inducing changes to airport security after September 11, such changes might look and sound effective or reassuring to the public, but their real-world effectiveness is doubtful.

Today's students are prodded, poked, profiled, analyzed, X-rayed, searched, and randomly drug-tested, all in the name of school security. Profiling students has become so invasive that there's even a growing national movement of school parents seeking to eliminate creative writing assignments in order to protect the private — and sometimes odd — thoughts of students from fanatical school administrators on the prowl for the next potential troublemaker.

This chapter examines some of the more glaring examples of this delusional exercise in educational paranoia sweeping our nation.

According to the American Civil Liberties Union, Matthew Parent, a seventeen-year old high school junior in Rhode Island, was suspended in 2000 for over a month as a result of his submission of an English class assignment.[40] Instructed to use a journal to engage in stream-of-consciousness creative writing exercises, he submitted nine handwritten pages. After reviewing the submission, Matthew's teacher showed the pages to a guidance counselor, who in turn passed it on to the school psychologist.

Without speaking to Matthew, the psychologist and a school social worker reviewed the material and advised the principal that there were "suicidal, homicidal, mood concerns, non-bizarre delusions of grandeur and narcissistic themes included in the exposition." The essay, they believed, exhibited "an enduring pattern of inner experience and behavior that deviates markedly from the expectations of his culture" and "significant distress and impairment in the academic setting."

Relying *exclusively* on the memo, and ignoring the fact that Matthew was well-behaved and receiving excellent grades in all his academic studies (including honors classes) the principal advised Matthew's mother that he would not be allowed to return to school without a psychological evaluation.

Obviously the people running this school haven't heard of a little thing called teen angst. (Note: Matthew was re-enrolled over a month later when the school settled a lawsuit filed by the family.)

Another case involved a third grader in Hudson, Ohio, who in 1998 was suspended for three days because of an allegedly threatening fortune she wrote as a class project to place in fortune cookies.[41] Her threat? "You will die with honor" was the fortune she submitted. Although the school reversed itself, the incident actually occurred, and a lawsuit was filed against the school district. One wonders if "suspended for threatening fortune cookie" still appears in her permanent record or not.

It's a sad day when over-zealous school administrators rush to judgment because something a student says or writes sounds malicious on the surface. Rather than look at the context of the situation or the student's past record and performance in the school, panicked and lazy administrators are quick to dole out suspensions and stigmatize students under a much-professed policy of zero-tolerance.

Even worse are school administrators quick to suspend students who speak their minds, even when it is on their own time and away from school grounds. While this can be seen as a form of censorship, it could have much more to do with school officials trying to keep their school's problems away from public view and from where they might be held accountable.

The very sad fact is that most students punished for speaking their minds are in fact voicing legitimate dissatisfaction with the school, especially if such concerns are ignored by school administrators when voiced through normal grievance channels. One notable example was sixteen-year old Brandon Beussink, suspended in 1998 after publishing a personal website critical of his school's poorly developed website and several school policies.[42] Nothing on Brandon's site was condoning violence or illegal activity, and he worked on the site from home — on his own computer — on his own time. The site simply encouraged visitors to e-mail school officials and complain about the issues he raised.

School administrators responded to Brandon's comments by suspending him for ten days and then failing him for the entire semester because of those absences. Although removing the site immediately after being contacted by school officials, he received no notice of his forthcoming punishment, and administrators denied his request to appeal the punishment. As his class prepared to graduate, Brandon had to re-earn all his credits from the previous semester, even though he completed all his classes and passed all his finals — all because he spoke out about problems at his school on his own time, on his personal website, using his home computer.

More saddening is a student at Belleview High School in Washington State who was suspended for ten days in 2000 because a personal website that he created using computers at a public library and hosted off-campus used vulgar language to criticize and insult his school.[43] Jim Wohrley, the school's principal, said that the student wasn't suspended for his opinions, but because he used foul language. "This is not about freedom of speech . . . it's a violation of the district's code of student conduct. When he brought the school's name into it, it brought it onto the school grounds."

That seems to be an excessively broad interpretation of a district's code. Next they'll mandate that all students bow their heads when uttering their school's name, no matter where they are saying it. How very Talibanish.

And, in 2001, Alex Smith, an honors student at a Michigan school, was suspended for writing a humorous commentary about his school's new tardiness policy.[44] The commentary, written at home and read aloud to a few friends there, criticized the policy, the process leading to its adoption, and several teachers and administrators charged with its enforcement. Although genuinely cooperative throughout the incident, he was suspended for ten days for committing "verbal assault" by allegedly "assaulting the dignity of a person" — from his living room at home.

Unreal.

Implementing a fanatical, "shoot first" zero-tolerance regimentation akin to prison life requiring mandatory conformity and stifling creativity is not the answer to the ills plaguing the majority of our public schools. I'm waiting for the day when all school students are given tranquilizers at the start of each school day to keep them in line and compliant.

Oh, wait . . . they already are. But that's discussed in another chapter.

Unchecked, these actions will produce future herds of mindless conformists happy to accept whatever they're told by an authority figure, because they're unable to think independently or creatively for themselves during the all-important formative years.

Then again, this might be what we intended to produce all along.

8

Cloistered Kids Syndrome

I have never let my schooling interfere with my education.
  - Mark Twain

I'm having a hard time trying to understand how our society will evolve over the coming decades. Not that it won't — rather, I'm wondering how our future will turn out when society is run by the products of today's over-protective, over-compensating parents.

If you remember, as children most of us learned to ride our bikes after the training wheels were removed, that is, with some tipping over, occasional bruising, but with a solid feeling of success when we finally managed to navigate a stretch of sidewalk without wobbling over. We listened when our parents told us which streets to avoid. When we got a little older, if we wanted to sleep over at a friend's house and use our bikes to travel there, we were directed to call our parents and let them know we arrived safely. We were told to avoid any cable television channel containing the word "Spice" because it contained inappropriate content for our young virgin eyes. Later, in high school, we'd grudgingly accept curfews and "check-in" phone calls in exchange for the ability to expand our social lives.

But thinking back, how many of us occasionally forget — intentionally or not — to call Mom when we got to our friend's house? And how many of us, as we got closer to adolescence, began to use the "forbidden streets" to get around town? How many late Saturday nights did Dad fall asleep in the

BarcaLounger (and awaken with fire in his eyes) when we came home far beyond our assigned curfew? Didn't we love going on overnight (and preferably co-ed) school trips where we could get the Spice Channel in the hotel room, and discovered why our parents didn't want us watching, or why co-ed trips were so much fun?

Part of growing up is testing one's limits, even if you know you will get in trouble if caught. In fact, the urge to do something forbidden generally rises with the penalties associated when you're caught doing it. Whether it's sneaking a glimpse of pornography, exploring an abandoned house in the neighborhood, going to a party you were forbidden to attend, bringing a girl into your bedroom for an innocent and passionate — but fully-clothed — "make out" session (for starters,) or driving to a town you were specifically told not to, these mini-rebellions make you feel like you're the one in charge — that you're the one making decisions about your destiny. And for a while, or until caught, *you* are the adult and are responsible for making decisions about your actions. More importantly, it's a critical and normal part of child development.

Traditionally, the teen years allow you to distinguish what you *can* do from what you *cannot* do, and — more importantly — what you *should* or *should not* do in a given situation. Such experiences establish how a person will face life and make decisions as an adult, particularly their ability to weigh the consequences of their decisions and actions.

Unfortunately it seems that my "Generation X" will be the last generation fortunate enough to have the opportunity to grow up normally, learn from personal mistakes, and gain trial-by-fire experience from our youth. While every generation frowns on the youth of the next, thanks to the rise in technology, Generation X is likely the last one that will know what having personal privacy and independence feels like as a minor, and having the privilege of learning things on their own.

Thanks to irrational parental fears — fueled by the media and companies hawking their wares — today's children and teenagers are nothing more than post-natal embryos being raised in carefully-controlled and monitored social environments that ensures nothing bad of any sort — from themselves or others — happens to them. (Granted, the same can be said of any generation looking at its successor, but technology sort of makes this a more salient distinction today.)

As British sociologist Frank Furedi notes in his book *Paranoid Parenting*, "In a loving environment, even a traumatic episode need not prevent a child from bouncing back and developing into a confident adult. However, if parents stifle their children with their obsessions and restrict their scope to explore, then the young generation will become socialized to believe that vulnerability is the natural state of affairs."[45]

Replacing the trials and lessons of childhood with a perfect pre-fab environment where nothing bad will ever happen may serve to reassure parents, but in the long run, it only decreases the capability of children to learn self-reliance and make good decisions. It also endangers their ability to function as future adults during strange or uncomfortable situations. Parents routinely want their children to take-control of their lives, but as you'll see, their actions are anything but supportive of that noble goal, especially when coupled with the dismal state of American education system.

Therefore, let's examine some of the features contributing to Cloistered Kids Syndrome:

Frightened that your child may be lost at a store, mall, or amusement park? Never fear! A $400 "family-management device" from Boston-based Wherify Wireless will put your mind at ease. Lock this tamper-proof wristwatch-sized device on your child — or hide a smaller-sized one in their backpack or on their clothing — and you've got a satellite-based Global Positioning System locator that can track your child's whereabouts or automatically alert you when children stray from parentally-established boundaries. (Incidentally, many modern cellular phones can be tracked as well, so when your child outgrows Wherify, you can still keep an eye on them.)

Want to ensure your teenager is becoming a responsible, safe driver? For a monthly fee, California-based Road Safety International will provide a "black box" for your family car that monitors how fast your teen drives, how sharp they make turns, or if they remember to fasten their seat belt before starting the car. And, for instant corrections, the device can emit increasingly louder sounds to annoy teen drivers when they exceed their parentally controlled limits when behind the wheel. Of course, back at home, parents can upload the contents of the "black box" to their PC and see how their teen driver is doing, and either praise or punish the kid accordingly. Some of these devices even include Global Positioning System features so parents can always know where their cars, and presumably their teens, are at any given time. All of this because, as an advertisement for a competing product reads, "your teenager doesn't have the wisdom of an adult yet. That's why he or she needs your close supervision and attention [provided by our product.]"[46] But you'll still put them behind the wheel of a deadly machine anyway. Go figure.

Concerned about what your child might see on television? Cable television provider Comcast actually developed a web document entitled *"How Do I Control What My Child Watches?"* describing the ways parents can restrict what channels their children can watch.[47] The company suggests parents consult their cable television user's guide for more guidance on this most important issue, but I've got a better suggestion: Get to know your kids and their interests, and instill in them a sense of responsibility about right and wrong in the context of what they are watching, instead of simply declaring (or having someone else declare) something "off limits." That's part of being a parent, isn't it?

Terrified that your child might learn about sexuality from someplace other than a classroom? Today, the Internet and the forbidden allure of online pornography have replaced the forbidden content of the Spice Channel and *Playboy*. But thanks to any number of companies, parents can install software to block sexually explicit sites, terms, or chat sessions that their children might encounter as they venture into cyberspace. Better yet, a parent can install software that monitors everything their child does while online. Forget about sitting down with your children and taking an interest in their online activities as a concerned parent. Besides, since talking to our kids about sex makes us uncomfortable, we'll just outsource yet another parental responsibility to a convenient third party. Not to mention, what they don't learn from us, they'll learn from school anyway. At least that's what parents hope.

I don't need to be a parent – and I'm not — to say confidently that technology can never replace good parenting.

Nobody buying into these "safety" schemes seems to understand that if a child is aware that their parents know where they are — or what they're doing — at any given moment and can monitor them minute-to-minute, they're creating a perfectly safe — and perfectly stunted — child. Stunted because this child never has the opportunity to disobey or try to circumvent parental rules and learn the true meaning of the term "consequence of their actions" — even if they get away with it. In the long term, this style of child rearing will produce an adult unable to make independent decisions, act under pressure, or function during a crisis because during their formative years, someone else made all the decisions for them. In effect, this sort of parenting will produce a perfect social drone that goes with the flow of society, afraid to deviate from its pre-planned programming.

In her December 2002 *Washington Post* feature on this growing problem, Laura Sessions Stepp pointed out, "We can all remember lessons in childhood that, though painful or scary at the time, taught us something useful: standing up to bullies, testing physical endurance, refusing to lie, risking failure in a tough course, getting back on the bicycle after a fall, learning how to handle a dictatorial teacher, acquiring the knowledge that life is not fair, easy, logical or as happy as Americans think it should be."[48]

It's gotten so bad that colleges now have counselors on-staff to help incoming students cope with the stress of freshman year when living on their own — presumably as adults, but based on what we are producing, more like high-school freshman, only with overactive hormones, unlimited credit cards, and their first taste of freedom.

Society has become so risk-averse that learning through mistakes or personal failure is no longer socially acceptable. Zero-tolerance is the new standard. At what point do people become able to take charge of their lives, make their own decisions, and learn from their experiences without the training wheels?

Unless this trend is reversed, and parents start being parents again, Cloistered Kids Syndrome will become Incapacitated Adulthood Condition. Not only is the latter next to impossible to treat; it's a very disturbing prospect for the future.

9

Functional Illiterates

Education is not to reform students or amuse them or to make them expert technicians. It is to unsettle their minds, widen their horizons, inflame their intellects, teach them to think straight, if possible.
- Robert M. Hutchins

There are plenty of things wrong with America's public schools. Everyone from politicians and pundits to op-ed writers has a laundry-list of issues, concerns and complaints about what the public schools are doing wrong. Therefore, for a complete change of pace I've decided to focus not on what schools are doing *wrong* — but on what they're not doing *at all*.

Schools are doing little to prepare our children for their futures. How's that for starters?

This statement is not aimed just at America's inner city schools — schools so dismal that in 2002 Congress enacted the "No Child Left Behind" policy. Rather, I'm talking about schools of *all* sizes and qualities, including the "good" public schools in nice middle-class communities. And while volumes are written annually questioning the quality of material being taught — a very real concern — this chapter is concerned with the sudden and fanatical injection of technology into our schools and its impact on education.

The Dot Com Boom of the 1990s contributed to a growing dependence on the "gee-whiz" factor of computers to coax, cajole, and entertain students on their path to graduation and higher education. This phenomenon was only encouraged by the 1996 enactment of the "E-Rate" offering schools partial or full subsidies for buying telecommunications services like Internet connection fees and wiring classrooms by charging a "Universal Service Fee tax on everyone else's phone bills.

To reinforce this perceived need, in his commencement address at MIT in 1998 President Clinton warned that "until every child has a computer in the classroom and the skills to use it . . . until every student can tap the enormous resources of the Internet . . .until every high-tech company can find skilled workers to fill its high-wage jobs . . . America will miss the full promise of the Information Age."[49]

Clinton's remarks only reinforced the unspoken belief that unless technology is used as often as possible during the school day, the faculty will fail their responsibilities as educators by not providing this "dynamic, interactive, exciting learning experience" for their students. As a result, more and more of the classes where students can explore their personal creativity are being replaced with technology-oriented, practical ones, and, if money allows, computers are used to teach traditional subjects like reading and math.

These days, Choir is out, 'Basic PowerPoint' is in. 'Using Microsoft Windows' replaces Art, and so on; the ability to use computer software to develop and exchange ideas is deemed more important than encouraging the exploration and nurturing of a student's native creativity.

Unfortunately for the future, today's schools are rearing a nation of *users* instead of critical *thinkers* or *creators*, encouraged by tax-deductible donations of computers and software from large technology companies holding a vested interest in seeing their products used to bring students — and future paying customers — into the Information Age. It's like a drug dealer offering free samples to a target market of future addicts. In this case, technology companies are preying on the serious economic shortcomings of our politicized public education system to peddle their wares and gain new, hopefully addicted, long-term customers.

To facilitate children's exposure to technology, some schools now issue laptops to all students or ensure that at least one class per day is in a computer laboratory. But a class is only fifty-minutes long — in the average fifty-minute class, how much time is wasted booting up these laptops, logging into the class network, and dealing with the usual assortment of technical hiccups, all too common with many of today's computers (especially Windows-based ones?) At best guess — and on a good day — this leaves about twenty minutes for any real education to occur on a variety of subjects that formerly were taught without the use of computers in the classroom.

And let's not ignore the fact that the computing activities of students in today's wired classrooms probably will be divided between class assignments (e.g., taking notes or downloading research material) and recreational pursuits (e.g., surfing the Internet, chatting, or checking personal e-mail) during class periods when the teacher isn't looking.

Gone are the days when students were brought into biology class to dissect frogs and earthworms; now there are computer programs that simulate in super-duper high-resolution what the innards of such creatures looks like. Students can point and click their way around the on-screen creature and use that virtual scalpel to slice and then open the frog's lower abdomen to reveal the digitized image of the gizzard; then they can virtually "inject" formaldehyde into their on-screen specimen to "preserve" it until the next day's class.

Dissecting a real specimen — cheap and populous as they are — was probably an affront to the People for the Ethical Treatment of Animals (PETA), or brought a school into the crosshairs of the kookier (and violent) Animal Liberation Front (ALF.) Using digital frogs allows schools to respect the rights of frogs to live in peace alongside people while avoiding any of the lab bombings ALF seems to find so satisfying in making their point. Plus, there's no sharp scalpel that could be used as a weapon by a potentially deranged student...and besides, touching frogs and worms is just icky, so why make students uncomfortable? This is a lawsuit-free solution!

In the next step up the educational science track are high school chemistry classes that now teach anything but real chemistry. Rather than being told not to mix acids and bases, marveling at the accidental flash of magnesium, or learning the old fashioned way about the stinky side-effect of sulfur, students learn the practical aspects of chemistry through computer simulations. On-screen beakers and flasks mix compounds, calculate molarities, and high-resolution animated bubbles show complex chemical reactions taking place in a safe, sterile, virtual environment.

But sometimes, you have to learn by doing. Simulating a chemical reaction isn't the same as doing the work and seeing the results for yourself, or accepting personal responsibility for *following directions* to ensure a safe experiment.

Now, the only danger posed to students in chemistry class is the computer crashing. Again, just like they did in biology, students point and click their way to a passing grade, and the school avoids lawsuits arising from any accidents or hurt feelings. Even though doing hands-on lab work can make science more interesting and enable a student to grasp what they can't by simply reading the textbook and clicking on a program, that doesn't seem to be the point anymore.

I dread the day when Driver's Ed is taught via CD-ROMs and computer simulation programs instead of by an experienced instructor with a second set of pedals and steering wheel in the passenger seat . . . and you should, too. Or sex-ed, for that matter. But then again, in today's litigious, risk-averse, faith-based society, how many school districts still offer it, anyway?

Elementary school students now get to do math homework on their Sony PlayStations instead of completing assignments full of boring equations and multiplication tables. Educational titles from LightSpan and other companies glue children to their televisions for homework and provide musical animated games to keep kids edu-tained outside the classroom.

"The kids love it. They're interested in it, and if you can get students where they think they're learning and they're playing, it has hit the magic mark," explained Joy Davis, assistant principal at Summerour Middle School in Georgia in a 2002 interview with CNN.[50]

Heaven forbid we force students to do something they don't like during their school years! After all, nothing in life should *ever* be uncomfortable or less than totally fun to participate in, right? What we forget amid all this gee-whiz edu-tainment is that nobody builds character or self-discipline by only doing what they like doing or are good at. Smooth seas do not a skilled sailor make.

Students don't visit the library for research anymore, they log onto the Internet. Granted, there is a wealth of useful material available online, but given their existing education — or level of common sense — how many students are able to determine if what they're downloading as research material is indeed accurate? Do students realize that a hastily-thrown-together website hosted for free — and by anyone in the world — at GeoCities probably doesn't have the same academic legitimacy or quality as a site hosted by a college think-tank, renowned scientist, or major research facility? Probably not. If it sounds good and is available on the Internet, it's a potential reference source and good enough for a paper.

What happens if a student's Internet connection is slow, or broken? Will the students know how to use the library to find information without first asking the librarian? Again, probably not – but this assumes schools keep hiring librarians rather then just assigning teachers to sit in the library and shush people during their free periods.

It's not better at the college level, either. Having taught advanced undergraduate college classes, I've graded student papers, and believe me when I say that a thousand chained monkeys pecking away on keyboards have a better command of written English than many of today's native-born American college students. This is mainly thanks to the abandonment of traditional English instruction and phonics, coupled with the rise of the feel-good, politically-correct abomination known as "social promotion" of students through the K-12 system.

Ask today's student — collegiate, high school, or elementary — to proofread a paper, and they'll fire up spell and grammar-checking software programs. Forget re-reading it with their own eyes or making the personal determination that *their* and *there* are not interchangeable terms; in the eyes of the spell-checking program, the words are spelled correctly and that's good enough for the students. Dangling your modifiers? Don't worry, Microsoft Word will correct it for you, and — better yet — you don't even need to know *what* a dangling modifier is! Technology will correct for you what you don't even know is wrong. As a result, I wonder if we're overcoming — or perpetuating — ignorance or if we're empowering — or enslaving — ourselves to the capabilities and limitations of technology.

Gone are the days where students had to take notes by pen and paper, and if they missed something had to raise their hand to ask for clarification from the teacher. Teachers are more then happy to join the technology revolution and now use PowerPoint slide shows to present material, and many allow students to download copies of the class slides for their notes.

What does this teach students about personal responsibility (such as staying awake, paying attention, and taking notes,) let alone the subject at hand?

Even elementary school students are expected to present class reports using Microsoft PowerPoint. Students using "old-fashioned" poster board, glue, and markers are frowned on by teachers and other students — despite the long hours and original thought put into their creations. The subtle lesson being taught in today's wired classrooms is that technology is the only way to express oneself and anything else is worthy of contempt.

If I were teaching middle school, I'd prefer to grade a project created with poster board, glue and glitter rather than PowerPoint anytime. That's true *creativity*, based — literally — on a blank sheet of paper and not a finite set of pre-programmed shapes, icons, and images on a computer screen from some commercial software package.

Unabated, and over time, this mindset will stifle students' creativity as they begin to believe that the colors, shapes, and templates contained in the software are the *only* possible choices they can choose from to develop their creation. In essence, they'll begin to lose their creative potential and ability to think for themselves in new and exciting ways.

There's no limit to what can be done with poster board; the same can't be said for PowerPoint. Not to mention, becoming dependent on PowerPoint makes students (and working professionals, for that matter) feel that *how* they present their information is more important than *what* they're actually saying, or how they arrived at that conclusion.

As Sherry Turkle, a professor at the Massachusetts Institute of Technology, noted in a January 2003 *Chicago Tribune* article, "PowerPoint is one of the most popular software systems in elementary and secondary schools. But PowerPoint doesn't teach children to make an argument. It teaches them to make a point, which is quite a different thing. It encourages presentation, not conversation. Students grow accustomed to not being challenged. A strong presentation is designed to close down debate, rather than open it up."[51]

It is a sad state of affairs that today's graduates who enter tomorrow's workforce are not only less educated than their parents but are unable to think outside the technology-derived boxes they've been reared in — assuming that they can even think for themselves, let alone do so critically.

As a result, they're less creative, less independent, and less capable as adults to contribute positively and responsibly to the challenges of the world around them. They're unable to seek answers for themselves or even have the visceral sense to know when something 'sounds' wrong and should be challenged.

But rest assured, they can send e-mail, cut-and-paste, run spell check, and synthesize papers from disparate sources that they didn't cite correctly.

Today's graduates are drones — simple, functional, task-oriented users. Or as my aunt — holder of a PhD and teacher of English for thirty-plus years in New York — calls them, "functional illiterates."

Ah, the wonders of technology. How did we live without it for so long?

(Note: This chapter may sound overly pompous or nostalgic; that is not my intention. Rather, I believe that more people from my "Generation X" have an idea about where to go about learning what they don't know beyond Google and the Internet, unlike today's students — and tomorrow's adults. I mean, for starters, at least we're familiar with the Dewey Decimal System and an Encyclopedia Britannica you can flip, not click, through. Many of us still have library cards, too. For that matter, how many of today's children – or adults - even know where their neighborhood library is located?)

10

Generation Rx

When I sell liquor, it's called bootlegging and made a crime; when my patrons serve it on Lake Shore Drive, it's called hospitality and made a business.
— Al Capone

Drugs and society. America's premiere love-hate relationship.

On one hand, we have the federal government's so-called War on Drugs working to eliminate the social dangers caused by illegal drug addicts. The public supports this program because illegal drugs are bad — or they wouldn't be illegal, right? Further, the American public is also led to believe and supports the notion because — as the Office of Drug Control Policy began promoting after September 11 — that buying illegal drugs is a *major* source of funding for international terrorism.

On the other hand, the federal government turns a blind eye when it's the American drug conglomerates that are pushing drugs on America's children. School officials and the public support this venture because it's been made clear to them that our children are disturbed and need help. Besides, buying drugs from American companies isn't only legal; it's good for American business.

The end result of this two-fold policy is the creation of a nation of overly medicated, addicted children, and a hypocritical national policy that leaves people shaking their heads and questioning what it is they're actually endorsing.

While many states have draconian laws in place to punish people for the tiniest amount of marijuana possession, if your child has tantrums, a limited attention span, poor social skills, is hyperactive, withdrawn, or disruptive in the classroom, a school counselor will inform you that your child has Attention Deficit Disorder (ADD) or Attention Deficit Hyperactive Disorder (ADHD) and would *greatly benefit* from any number of psychotropic curatives (such as Ritalin or Cyclert) being pimped out to the school by America's leading drug companies.

If a diagnosis of ADD or ADHD has been placed on your child's school record, chances are you'll be told that you can't enroll your child in public school unless you sign a waiver allowing the school nurse to supply them with their Drug of The Day. And, according to the *New York Post*, if you refuse to start or continue medicating your child (either on principle or because you noticed side-effects from the drugs, such as psychotic mood swings) you will be reported to Child Protective Services as a "bad parent" by school administrators.[52]

Comply with the medicating program, and you'll notice (in the majority of cases) that your child will become more docile, complacent, sit still for extended periods of time, and not cause disruptions in school — or anywhere else for that matter — almost overnight.

Teachers are happy and you're thrilled. You might pat yourself on the back for being a responsible parent and taking good care of your child. But are you really helping your child, or just turning her or him into a legally sanctioned drug addict?

Although a growing number of experts are beginning to admit that children undergoing normal development are being drugged into submission by people who don't have any idea of what they're doing and don't understand children, the public is being inundated with the image of the "ideal child" — one that is quiet, docile, focused, attentive, and less hyperactive. Of course, as luck would have it, the drug companies have solutions readily at hand to help society achieve this desired goal. Better yet, doctors are more then willing to dole out prescriptions at an exponential rate — and everyone knows that if a *doctor* prescribes something, it *must* be safe.

So if a child is bored in the classroom, the answer is to drug them. Pay no attention to the fact that the child may not be grasping the material or may have already mastered it. If a child needs to learn at a different pace or is a "free spirit" who interrupts class with questions, just hand them a pill and they will sit docilely without interrupting the teacher. Thanks to a few magical meds, a child who might be acting out due to undiagnosed problems that need addressing — such as a sight or hearing problem — will no longer be a burden to the classroom, or their parents either.

Talk about a mind-numbing problem.

What we're seeing is a growing reluctance to confront children's pain and troubles because it's just cheaper and easier to medicate them away. Even though it's part of their responsibilities, parents, teachers, coaches, mentors, and counselors are simply too busy or unwilling to provide the individual attention many children need, want, and deserve as they mature. Just pop a few pills and the problem is suppressed. No muss, no fuss, and it's probably tax-deductible. Another benefit of the Era of Instant Gratification!

Thanks to the massive amounts of psychotropic drugs being fed to our children, we're raising a generation unable to question, unable to think clearly, and essentially unable to function. In effect we are creating cookie-cutter Stepford children: they sit straight, look great, never cause a scene and never get dirty. These children may be the epitome of "normal" as defined by school administrators and pharmaceutical companies, but as a result, they'll never learn to be self-directed, independent individuals or competent future adults.

But perhaps the Stepford child is the desired result, especially if you think about who actually benefits from creating a nation of zoned-out children.

The children certainly don't benefit. Rather, it's the *teachers* who aren't sure how to handle normally developing students; *parents* who are tired of complaints from teachers and dealing with the responsibilities of parenthood; *school officials* looking to keep their schools safe and avoid lawsuits; *doctors* who make money each time a child comes in for a refill; and the *companies* that manufacture, market, and sell these drugs at high profit margins.

Medical research firm IMS Health reported that about 20 million prescriptions for Ritalin-type drugs were dispensed in 2000, compared to the 14 million prescriptions dispensed in 1996.[53] That same year, the U.S. Census Bureau reported that there were 281 million people in America. Of that total, 72 million, or 26 percent of America's population, were under the age of 18.[54]

Are we to believe that almost *one-quarter* of America's youth is being drugged into submission each day? And are we to believe that there's *nothing* wrong with this?

Ritalin, one of the most popular and addictive drugs being doled out to children, was reported by the Drug Enforcement Administration to have had a 700% increase in use during the 1990s.[55] But Ritalin is considered so powerful by the FDA that it's illegal to test this type of drug on children.

The logic here defies belief — although we can't legally test Ritalin on children, we continue to medicate millions of them with it daily. And when ADD or ADHD isn't as profitable as it is now, you can bet a new crop of childhood "conditions" will suddenly require pharmaceutical drug treatment. Heck, they're starting to run television commercials targeting *Adult*

Attention Deficit Disorder – something unheard of two years ago — as part of the drug industry's marketing plan to ensure profitability from Generation Rx after it graduates high school. Clinical depression is just so passé these days.

In our brave new world, a child can spend almost his or her entire life in a haze of legally-sanctioned and prescribed drugs that effectively alters their innate talents and curiosity about the world around them just so they can conform to modern society's fantasy of what a "normal" child should be like.

This runaway medication of children — used as a substitute for therapy and in the absence of any other intervention or attention — has become an uncontrolled national experiment with still-unknown consequences, both to the children now, and to our society as they become adults in the future.

And we're still worried about marijuana use?

11

God, Inc.

It is hard to say whether the doctors of law or divinity have made the greater advances in the lucrative business of mystery.
– Edmund Burke

I'm not afraid to say that organized religion — especially many sects of Christianity — doesn't impress me anymore.

Sure, they all generally preach peace, love, equality, and happiness, but that's only under the guise of providing points for the afterlife by appealing to people who are desperate for some form of hope in troubled times. However, in the here and now, religion is the cause of war, death, genocide, social subjugation, censorship, and any other number of bad things around the world, all sold to the faithful as God's will. If you don't believe me, check out what's been happening in Afghanistan, Saudi Arabia, Israel, Iran, Nigeria, Iraq, and any other number of hot spots across the globe today, including, to a lesser degree, the United States.

Although raised Catholic, in my adult life, I came to believe that no "God" that I felt comfortable worshipping would tolerate such things, or constrain followers to a dogmatic set of rules, regulations, and subjugations that restrict their abilities to flourish as people to their fullest potential. If anything's going to happen to me in my life, it's going to do so because of what *I* choose to do or not do. I alone am responsible for how my life is lived.

It's *not* God's fault if my house crumbles in an earthquake — it's my fault for building it on a fault line and not listening to the engineer doing the land survey. It's *not* God's fault if I get into an automobile accident; for that I've got only myself to thank or blame. It's also *not* God's fault if I get sick or develop some sort of disease; for that I've got my environment or possibly heredity to thank or blame. And, when I die, it's *not* God 'calling me home' to be with Him, it's Nature taking its course with me.

Being raised Christian, I've got the most experience with that set of beliefs, even though I've observed other mainstream beliefs as well. As such, my remarks on organized religion are based on my observations of Christianity over the years, and helps explain both why I'm disgusted and amazed that the Catholic Church in particular, continues to survive in the world.

What really strikes me is that while Christianity proudly claims its leaders take a vaunted oath of poverty, its actions over the years — Mother Theresa aside — show otherwise.

Consider the recently built Los Angeles Cathedral, otherwise known by city residents as the "Taj Mahoney" in satirical honor of Cardinal Mahoney who's in residence there. The building cost over a hundred million dollars to build and is perhaps the ugliest structure in the entire city. The money used to build it could have eradicated the city's entire homeless problem forever, but instead was used to erect a testament to a clergyman who did everything in his power to cover up the pedophile problem plaguing his area of the American Catholic Church.

That's not living in poverty, but a demonstration of hypocrisy. And in the Bible, Jesus reserved some of his harshest criticisms for the hypocrites. But never mind the facts, or the revivalist question "what would Jesus do?" — please keep the faith and keep giving, because the Catholic Church sure needs funds to survive in this new millennium of lawsuits and lavish luxury.

Or rather, the *business* of Church needs funds, because that's all it is really is; namely, the business of social control. After all, Napoleon Bonaparte once quipped that religion is something made by men and it is "excellent for keeping the common people quiet."

If you think about it — and can see past the ornate buildings, choirs, statues and stained glass — the organized religions of the world are nothing more than global enterprises that provide feel-good promises (i.e., services) with the ultimate goal of separating you from your money while trying to keep you as a loyal customer of their brand name.

But in most cases, "God" is just a marketing idea used to establish brand identity. Reverends, ministers, deacons, and priests are just another name for sales executives, account managers, and consultants who market products in a very competitive market and try to break into new ones while keeping their churn rate down. Ask any marketing executive; they'll tell you it's all about "branding."

And organized religion is no different.

To illustrate this point, let's compare the Catholic Church (a mainstream organized religion) with Microsoft (a publicly-traded technology company) and see where the similarities are between these two global enterprises. Let the evidence speak for itself:

BUSINESS TYPE

Microsoft: A for-profit corporation headquartered in Redmond, Washington State, with offices in nearly every country around the world, legions of endorsed (vendor-certified) consultants, and evangelists to market how Microsoft can empower you or your business in its quest for world dominance. Although not a sovereign territory with a seat at the United Nations, its international influence and close ties with the United States and other governments practically makes it a sovereign territory. Private security forces patrol its headquarters site and escort its executive management while on travel.

Catholic Church: A non-profit corporation headquartered in the sovereign territory of Vatican City, located in the heart of Rome, Italy, supported by multiple branch offices in population centers around the world with legions of officially endorsed (ordained) employees and tolerated (evangelist) consultants to market their God concept and achieve dominance over the world's spiritual, moral, and social spheres. As a sovereign territory, the Vatican has diplomatic representation in the United Nations. Private security forces — the colorful Swiss Guards — patrol its headquarters site and escort its executive management while on travel (sans colorful attire.)

TICKER SYMBOL

Microsoft: NASDAQ – MSFT

Catholic Church: Not traded publicly, although "IGOD" was once considered as its ticker symbol on the Rome Exchange.

GOODS OR SERVICES OFFERED

Microsoft: Computer software, hardware products, Internet services and consulting to empower people in the Information Age based on the evolving nature and needs of technology and its users.

Catholic Church: Guidance on how it believes man can get into the afterlife (something they call "heaven") drawn from a narrow interpretation of what man *thinks* he heard God say at some point that sounded promising as he wandered around what's now the Middle East.

COMPANY SLOGAN

Microsoft: "Where Do You Want To Go Today?"

Catholic Church: "Got Guilt?" (Was previously the centuries-old "Got Indulgences?") Reportedly being considered as replacements in 2003 are "Don't Sue!" and "Got Forgiveness?"

CORPORATE LEADERSHIP

Microsoft: A chief executive officer (appointed by and serving at the pleasure of the board), his executive management, and a board of directors. All have signed corporate non-disclosure agreements regarding what they are exposed to or discuss in their respective roles with Microsoft. There are occasionally outside directors that sit on the Microsoft board, and its financial records are audited annually by an external auditing firm and made public.

Catholic Church: A Pope (appointed for life), his Cardinals, regional Archbishops, and Bishops. All have been sworn to secrecy regarding what they are exposed to or discuss in their respective roles with the Church. The Church does not have any outside Directors or auditors, and most records are kept secret. In order to maintain financial secrecy – and so the Pope can cash checks without a PopeMobile Driver's License — it even has its own private national bank.

SOURCES OF REVENUE

Microsoft: Selling and licensing products to customers, and inducing them to upgrade often. Providing technical consulting services to help customers deploy and use Microsoft products for the long-term (e.g., creating a dependency.) They also have a fee-based telephone help line — a highly effective source of income during hard economic times.

Catholic Church: Weekly and annually recurring pay-per-view events that dispense man's interpretation of what he thought he heard God say. (A necessity, since its highly profitable Retail Indulgences Group was eliminated after the Renaissance.) The Church also provides professional consulting services for social situations such as weddings, funerals, and periods of intense personal guilt where its customers want to chat with someone anonymously — fees vary based on the event and person's needs. The Church also supports local operations through the rental of parish halls for social gatherings and bingo tournaments. The object of these activities is to assist its customers seek out and rely on its suite of service offerings over the long-term (e.g., creating a dependency.)

PROPRIETARY INFORMATION

Microsoft: The source code — the "inner workings" of its flagship Windows product — is a closely guarded secret. Revealing it would allow competitors to see how its products work and are cobbled together. The company has worked diligently to keep this information away from the public eye for over twenty years. Thus, the firm creates a worldwide mass of faith-based followers despite what the reality of its products and history may be.

Catholic Church: Key documents in the Church's vaults include ancient records of how many people it killed during its many Crusades to spread its God's message to the world as well as copies of ancient scriptures that both support and contradict its institutional legitimacy. Keeping such things secret (as it's done for nearly two millennia) ensures that the Church will appear as moral and peaceful as it claims to be in its marketing materials. Thus, the firm creates a worldwide mass of faith-based followers despite what the reality of its products and history may be.

LEGAL PROBLEMS

Microsoft: Anti-trust suits arising from unfair business practices, in which a court found the company guilty of being a monopoly. The company was also caught deleting e-mail messages from corporate systems to preserve the institution during its legal proceedings, and acting as if it was beyond the reach of federal law.

Catholic Church: Anti-trust of another sort — namely that many of its employees can't be trusted to keep their cassocks on when they're around children. Like so many large corporations in recent years, Church officials routinely decide to conceal such transgressions to ensure the survivability of the organization instead of complying with codes of law in the communities where such transgressions occurred. Essentially — and quite arrogantly — the Church places itself above the laws of the people, claiming the supremacy of God's law. Except, of course, when such laws will help, such as the November 2002, decision by the Diocese of Boston to consider declaring bankruptcy under American civil law to preclude its having to pay lawsuit settlements arising from its pedophile scandals while at the same time keeping its secrets safe.

CORPORATE ACCOUNTABILITY

Microsoft: Accountable to its board of directors, shareholders, and any number of international regulatory organizations and laws. Information about any transgressions is made publicly accessible in court documents. Annoying, sure ... but it's the law.

Catholic Church: Accountable to itself, and all information regarding any improprieties falls under its Pontifical Secret Rules of Evidence. Should that fail, it will look to its God for guidance, and there is a high probability that He will agree with its need for secrecy. How very convenient.

ABILITY TO MEET CHANGING CUSTOMER INTERESTS

Microsoft: Recognizing the potential of the Internet to change the world, Chairman Bill Gates decreed in 1995 that — for better or worse — all Microsoft products would become network-centric to take advantage of the Information Revolution. The company has since embarked on a crash-course to reinvent itself as an Internet-services company to survive in this environment.

Catholic Church: Although dominated by male-only management and endorsed consultants, it refuses to adapt to the changing desires and needs of its customer base. One example is its steadfast refusal to allow women to serve as officially endorsed consultants (ordained clergy) despite their interest and the declining numbers of men in such roles. Another is the belief that since all life is sacred, a mother should die with her unborn child instead of allowing the child to die in order to save the mother's life and return her to society. After all, God would want it that way, even though modern social expectations are to the contrary.

WARRANTY OR GUARANTEES PROVIDED

Microsoft: Use our products at your own risk, and not in nuclear power plants, airplanes, or hospitals. You can try to sue us if you experience problems, but our lawyers are better dressed, better paid, and better connected than your lawyers, so you might want to think twice. Just keep buying our products and trust us.

Catholic Church: Live by our standards, and we'll promise you entry into that thing we like to call "heaven." Unfortunately, since nobody's come back from there to confirm this, you'll have to take our word on this. We offer no guarantees — just have faith that things will work out for you. Besides, given the expert witness he can summon, do you really think you can sue the Pope and win? Just keep giving us money and trust us.

The similarities between Microsoft and the Catholic Church, as you might have noticed are eerily similar, and should raise some questions about how seriously we should take what the Church — or Microsoft, for that matter — spokespeople say publicly, and how deeply we "buy into" their marketing pitches. It also begs the question about how the Church should adapt to meet the evolving needs of its congregations.

But the Church won't change. After all, its job is to change others, not change itself.

That being said, the Church's marketing material is quite correct in one area: It does have a good "Shepard" and its congregations are happy to serve as the mindless, revenue-generating flocks of "sheep" in its global herd. Indeed, as Karl Marx wrote, religion does serve as the addictive opiate of the masses.

And for the Church, that's not a *baaaaad* thing at all — and it's great for business!

12

Interpreting the Ten Commandments in 2003

A man's ethical behavior should be based effectually on sympathy, education, and social ties; no religious basis is necessary. Man would indeed be in a poor way if he had to be restrained by fear of punishment and hope of reward after death.
- Albert Einstein

Some believe the Bible doesn't really *say* anything, but rather it's how we interpret and apply what's contained within in our daily lives that makes it such a significant book.

As a litmus test to see if this is a valid statement or just baseless atheistic propaganda, let's take a look at the vaunted Ten Commandments — a prominent document found in several major world religions that was published on a mountain with (luckily) no witnesses — and apply them to the present-day world of 2003.

I. I AM THE LORD THY GOD, THOU SHALT NOT HAVE STRANGE GODS BEFORE ME

If you ever wondered why the world is as messed up as it is (and has been for several millennia) this one explains a great deal.

Instead of realizing this statement as a series of Universal Truths, most religions take a narrow, dogmatic path that preaches that their "God" is the only "God" — setting the stage for religious conflicts between ideologies competing for converts, collections, and legions of brainwashed followers who can *only* acknowledge their own dogmatic interpretations of their beliefs. With so many "Gods" competing for status as the *only true God* in the world, it's no wonder that more people throughout history have been killed in the name of religion than for any other reason.

(Note: In the Roman Catholic interpretation of the Decalogue, this Commandment is simply to justify and ensure God's monopoly status in the world. Added at the request of the heavenly lawyers at the Burning Bush office of Halo, Harpe & Cloude LLP.)

II. THOU SHALT NOT TAKE THE NAME OF THE LORD THY GOD IN VAIN

What do you want to do, start a war or something? National leaders invoking "God" to bless their nations and the raging debates over how (or even if) one can mention "God" in a government facility or public school only adds to the allure and brand-name reinforcement of organized religion as an absolute influence on society, and thus lays the foundation for religious-oriented social and military conflict.

As such, the mainstream religions of the world have millions of followers generally unable to take a momentary step back from their own views to consider — or even acknowledge — alternative views on religion. This has the unfortunate effect of turning anyone daring to offer competing views on religion into the object of heated enmity from all corners of the faith-based spectrum, something that Minnesota governor Jesse Ventura discovered a few years ago after sharing his personal belief that organized religions were a "crutch for weak-minded people." As a Realist, I tend to agree.

III. THOU SHALL REMEMBER THE SABBATH AND KEEP IT HOLY

This is pure commercialism — it's religion's roundabout way of saying, "stay tuned for the next exciting episode" of their weekly pay-per-view live events. You didn't think it was only the World Wrestling Federation that did live shows, did you? Where do you think they got the idea? How about "Must-See Television?" The Church was saying it long before NBC.

Those professing a belief in earth-based religions — heathens or pagans to some — believe that the concept of a deity is everywhere. They find God, Goddess, deity, and spirituality in their own manner, yet their moral views practically mirror those of mainstream religions. *Every* day is holy to them and, unlike organized religions, their faith generally isn't centered around expensive, ornate buildings with posted hours of operation, dogmatic worship guidelines, or a required weekly revenue stream. When they do have a ceremony, it's a gathering among *equals*, not appointed clergy dispensing dogma to the masses. As a result, these folks tend to be among the more tolerant and enlightened members of society — even if, at times, a little eclectic.

IV. HONOR THY FATHER AND THY MOTHER

While we should certainly honor and thank our parents for giving us life, if they fail in their roles as parents in preparing us to become competent future adults, do we really owe them beyond that? In some cases, yes.

Respect needs to be *earned* through actions and deeds that warrant it, not mandated through blind directives and brainwashing. Under this Commandment, an abused child must always respect and honor their parents, beatings or no beatings. That's not only wrong, but contradicts the good of the child, his or her development, and society in general. In some situations, it's a blessing that although someone couldn't pick their parents, they're able to pick their friends, some of whom might be closer to them than their own family.

No wonder all national leaders invoke His name in speeches — this Commandment shows God as the best friend of all politicians: Be docile and compliant. God says so. You can't argue with that logic, right?

V. THOU SHALT NOT KILL

Unless someone says their "God" is better than yours, or believes in something other than what you do — then it's okay to whack 'em. Just think about what the Christian Persecution, Crusades, Burning Times, Spanish Inquisition, the Reformation, the Huguenot War, the conflict in Northern Ireland, Jewish Holocaust, and Islamic Extremism — among others — were (and are) all about.

After all, there are those who believe that any form of life is a sacred gift, and that in some situations, God feels it's better for an adult woman to die rather than kill her unborn child — and if she's got other children, creating a few needy orphans (to be cared for by society) instead of their mother is morally-preferable to an abortion. Or, if the woman was impregnated against her wishes, she's to accept her new child as a gift from God provided under "trying circumstances," be forced to raise it, and thus become bound by an archaic interpretation of Christian dogma that's one step above Islamic Fundamentalism's views of women.

VI. THOU SHALT NOT COMMIT ADULTERY

Unless you have an attractive White House intern, that is. Just remember to have a competent dry cleaning service standing by before conducting her weekly performance reviews, and to receive moral counseling on the matter from a minister who engages in similar practices but hasn't been discovered yet.

This one sort of makes sense — after all, it's highly disruptive to the society for those who are pledged faithful to each other to be cheating when their partner's not around, especially since interpersonal trust is an integral part of society. After all, possession is nine-tenths of the law, right? However, if both people involved agree it's okay and willingly embrace such activities – and additional partners — as part of their sexual practice, that's another story...I've got no problem with that, if that's your thing.

VII. THOU SHALT NOT STEAL

... unless it's from your employee's 401(k) and you can get away fast enough.

And, in the eyes of the Catholic Church, it's not stealing — and certainly not hypocrisy — if instead of taking care of a city's homeless problem, it spends millions of dollars on an opulent new Cathedral simply to praise itself and ensure its survival in the region.

VIII. THOU SHALT NOT BEAR FALSE WITNESS AGAINST THY NEIGHBOR

In other words, don't lie unless you can get away with it, or make a very convincing argument of why it was necessary to lie at all. And if they accuse you, simply turn around and make it known that their "God" is not the true "God" that you believe in, and their remarks mean nothing to you because of this most disturbing fact.

Of course, you could always take the Fifth or claim Pontifical Secrecy. That works pretty well, or so I hear.

IX. THOU SHALT NOT COVET THY NEIGHBOR'S WIFE

This one is just stupid. If you're attracted to a woman, you're not sinning, you're human. Otherwise, why did God invent bare mid-drifts, tight leather jeans, and attractive females? Adam would've ogled Eve's twin sister — the Heavenly Hooters Girl — if she wasn't too busy interning for Heaven's Gatekeeper after she got off work as a landscaper in the Garden of Eden's apple orchard. Now, if you carry through with your desires, that's another story . . . but desire in and of itself isn't necessarily a bad thing.

X. THOU SHALT NOT COVET THY NEIGHBOR'S GOODS

In the case of your neighbor's goods, it's human nature to be envious of the new SUV or home theater system. As George Carlin says, consumer envy is good for the economy and ultimately helps your fellow man. By your desire to own what your neighbor has, you're employing other humans who manufacture and market such goods and thus receive a salary they can live on — which means that through your envy and purchasing ability, you demonstrate your compassion and love for your neighbor's well-being. God would want that, wouldn't He?

So what do *you* think?

As for me, I think that Sigmund Freud's observation that "when a man is freed of religion, he has a better chance to live a normal and wholesome life" isn't as diabolical or heretical as it sounds.

Either that, or we need to start re-evaluating how much emphasis we and our elected leaders place on religion in our modern society. I know I have.

13

America's Religious Wrong

At least two-thirds of our miseries spring from human stupidity, human malice and those great motivators and justifiers of malice and stupidity: idealism, dogmatism and proselytizing zeal on behalf of religious or political ideas.
- Aldous Huxley

Being a good citizen – let alone a functional person in society — carries with it the responsibility to stay informed, and that means being entitled to see and consider all sides of an issue — no matter how controversial — before making an informed decision for yourself. After all, the ability of an individual to explore, choose, and forge their own destiny is the epitome of what liberty and freedom are all about.

Unfortunately, it's a sad fact that the determination of what constitutes *appropriate* information in American society today rests not with the individual and their inquisitive mind. No, America is happy to delegate and outsource the social approval of books, movies, literature, and social policies — in other words, *acceptable* knowledge — to the private sector through the religious zealotry of various religions, most notably the Religious Right. Anything veering from their standards is subject to attack by lawsuit before eternal damnation, even if it's only to acknowledge a different point of view.

And, though the politically-correct (PC) left has its claws in America's values too, this discussion will focus on these organized — and often extremist — religious folks and their ministrations, since in many cases, religion is *the* major weapon in the war against reality around the world. Some — including myself — even call it the Ultimate Weapon of Mass Delusion.

The Religious Right has one goal, it seems — the moral cleansing of American society according to its generally medieval interpretation of Christianity's principles. After all, in the gospel of Matthew, Jesus allegedly told his followers to "make disciples of all nations, baptizing them in the name of the Father and of the Son and of the Holy Spirit, and teach them to obey everything I have commanded you." The Religious Right tries to do that – and then some.

Through their lobbying efforts, the term "family values" has come to mean a heterosexual relationship between men and women and sex only within marriage with the goal of raising a child, not for ongoing physical pleasure between married couples — thus meaning that anything that facilitates other (or frequent) sexual activities such as abortion, condoms, or contraceptives is a tool of sin. It's sex only after marriage; the knowledge or conduct of anything else is sinful and must be eliminated from society.

One wonders when they're going to propose that all American women cover themselves in a head-to-toe burkha like the women in Afghanistan under the Taliban.

As a result of years of lobbying by these so-called "family-values" organizations, we're stuck in a society with a significant lack of understanding of the world around it, or even with the ability to learn about anything other than "acceptable" perspectives on social issues, personal creativity, or humanity in general.

Self-appointed (or anointed, as the case may be) "family values" organizations like *Concerned Women for America*, the *Traditional Values Coalition*, the *American Family Association (AFA)*, and *Focus on the Family* routinely seek to remove from classrooms, libraries, television, movies, games, and society anything that they believe conflict with their beliefs. Forget religious tolerance, it's their God you better not offend or you're going to be smitten with an Almighty Lawsuit or buried in their incessant fire-and-brimstone public statements.

But that's okay, it seems, because in the eyes of these zealots even acknowledging alternative ideas or perspectives is akin to condoning it, and thus necessitates their quest to cleanse, cleanse, cleanse away anything other than what they think *their* God would approve of.

This approved national censorship movement seems to be gaining momentum with each passing year. And politics being what it is, our elected leaders are more than happy to cater to these groups, since doing otherwise puts them at risk for public vilification when the next election comes around. In other words, catering to these groups is a matter of job security for politicians.

To show how goofy some of these groups can get, one organization — the *Citizens for Community Values in Cincinnati* — is mobilizing against major hotel chains to stop them from offering pay-per-view pornography movies in guest rooms, saying it's easy access for anyone adults or children — to be exposed to illicit and immoral acts that might tempt them into committing sinful acts against their interpretation of the Bible.[56] The fact that many non-Christians might want to view such material is of no consequence to their position on the matter, or the reality that if a human being — of any age — wants sexual gratification, they're going to find a way to get it, even if it's by himself. Or herself.

We've seen the Religious-Right-leaning second Bush administration establish a White House Director of Faith-Based Programs to appease these religious groups and administer the President's faith-based "Compassionate Conservatism" programs promised during his 2000 campaign. Despite the legal mumbo-jumbo, the separation of religion and government must not apply to repaying support for Presidential campaigns.

Then, in 2002, the Religious Right successfully lobbied the federal government to remove fact sheets on "the effectiveness of condoms" and a sex education curriculum called "Programs that Work" from the websites for National Institute of Health (NIH) and the Centers for Disease Control and Prevention (CDC.)[57] Of course, they continue their quest to outlaw abortion under any circumstance, claiming it's an unholy action against a living being and a direct affront to their particular set of moral principles. To them, public opinion, human nature, and man-made laws are subordinate to their medieval religious dogma.

I say if these Christian mullahs don't like what they see in the world around them, they should move to the Vatican — or wherever they call their spiritual home — and live a quiet, cloistered life according to whatever dogma they like. Religious principles should *guide*, not control or unduly influence, morals and society.

Soon after this fiasco, Democratic Congressman Henry Waxman challenged the growing religious influence on government-provided information when he noted in December 2002, that "information that used to be based on science is being systematically removed from the public when it conflicts with the administration's political agenda."[58] Of course, the Bush administration — still catering to the Religious Right — denied any wrongdoing or political posturing in this matter.

And I should point out that this is happening in America, not Iran, Iraq, Saudi Arabia, Afghanistan, or any of the other countries our politicians foam at the mouth over for their religious-based "censorship" — because we are, after all, a nation that prides itself on church-state separation.

But when it comes to church-state separation, what we say and do are two different things, particularly in our public schools. Thanks to the efforts of the Religious Right's Thought Police, America's public school system continues to display increasing mixes of insane political correctness and religious censorship with each new school year. Obviously, this is done to shield America's youth from anything but a dogmatic view of Religious Right-leaning principles and make it difficult for students to examine any differing views as they learn about the world they're growing up in — at least while present on government-funded (and thus Religious Right-influenced) school facilities.

For example — do you want to write a book, record an album, or develop a television show or movie geared for (and marketed to) children? You'd better conform to a few simple rules cobbled together by the political correctness groups and the Religious Right's Thought Police — otherwise, you'll become the latest victim in their moral cleansing efforts.

The rules are simple: You may not show the world as it really is — both beautiful and ugly, loving and hating, happy and sorrowful. You may not depict adolescence as anything other than a period of beautiful learning or innocent wonderment prior to adulthood. You may not use bad language, sexual innuendo, or mention anything 'too' violent...after all, the *real* world isn't like that, right?

If you talk about any of the forbidden topics — particularly the normal sexual development or curiosity of a teenager — you're just begging the Religious Right's Thought Police to put your book, movie, or album on a list of *unacceptable* entertainment and stand a good chance of being boycotted by many "family values friendly" places like Wal-Mart unless you release a cleaned-up version for them to sell.

And spurred on by its success over the past few decades, the Religious Right's Thought Police are thinking in greater terms these days. Rather then confining their zealotry at the elementary and high school levels — colleges are now seen as prime targets as well.

In late 2002, the University of North Carolina (UNC) was sued by the *Family Policy Network (FPN)* — another Religious

Right-oriented "family values" group — for requiring incoming freshmen to read a book on Islam and then participate, if they chose, in discussion groups to explore the topic.[59] In their suit, the zealots at FPN claimed UNC, as a publicly-funded school, was "violating the separation of church and state" by "forcing students to submit" to the teachings of a particular religion, and one that at the time — shortly after September 11 — was seen by many Americans in a negative light.

Forget exposing students to a variety of new ideas, values, and cultures present in the real world. No, the Religious Right is content to press, and force whenever and wherever possible, their narrow vision of the world; a world of very particular beliefs with everything set between good and evil, God and Satan. One wonders if the FPN would have sued if UNC required students to submit to the study of Judaism or Christianity instead of Islam. I think not.

How can any educational institution — or country — pride itself on academic freedom when forced to restrict the breadth of information its students can be exposed to? If we're content to churn out college graduates that see the world through tunnel-vision according to a singular religious, national, or ideological perspective, what does that say about their ability to understand or learn new cultures, ideas, or values elsewhere in the world as they become our future leaders and have to deal with them? One only has to look at the type of education received in Saudi Arabian or Pakistani madrazzas to see this in action.

Despite the dearth of common sense in America today, I'm sure that college students can differentiate between reading a required book for class discussion and being subjected to brainwashing, as UNC's Chancellor told an audience at the National Press Club in Washington, DC.[60] Students can understand that reading a book on Islam for a class assignment isn't going to make them instant card-carrying members of Lucifer's Evil Minions.

Fortunately, the lawsuit was dismissed when a federal appeals court upheld the ruling that the summer reading saying that it didn't see a correlation between indoctrination and asking students to voluntarily read a book on Islam.[61]

In other words, despite FPN's threats to continue fighting the decision, the court told the mullahs of the Religious Right's Thought Police to bugger off. And rightfully so.

If only that was the end, but the Religious Right isn't content to focus their censorship policies only at schools where, as we just saw, they sometimes lose their battle. Their vision of societal cleansing covers all matters of society including entertainment. In nowhere more blatant do we see this than with every new release in the *"Harry Potter"* book series — a literary fantasy that has children not only excited about reading, but so excited they have been known to beg their parents to stand on long lines at midnight in order to get a copy as soon as possible.

So what if *"Harry Potter"* is a fantasy about magic? Parents know the subject of the book is fantasy and not religious proselytizing yet happily buy the books — most likely in a state of shock that their children were excited to read, which helps explain those midnight lines at bookstores around the world.

The fantasy genre is appropriate for the specified age group, and studies have shown that if children learn to enjoy reading when they are young, they will enjoy it for life, especially since reading helps children develop necessary skills of critical analysis and creative thinking.

This isn't a rock concert and it wasn't the work of Satan or witches seeking to promote their craft — it is a *book*. These kids are excited about escaping the crazy commercialized world around them for a few hours (or days) while reading something other than the lyrics of an Eminem album.

The night Harry Potter books go on sale, educators and parents observe something very special. Suddenly, in the fast-paced world of Dot-Com-This and Interactive-That, children drop their keyboards, turn off their cell phones, rush home from school, or beg to stay up late under the blankets with a flashlight to enjoy a book and the wonderment of reading.

With regard to children's books, if a talking pig and spider are permissible, and a little girl falling into a hole with odd and creepy characters teasing her for 200-plus pages while she becomes more and more unhinged passes muster, fantasy magic and a flying broomstick should be perfectly acceptable. Does anyone remember the Wicked Witch in the Wizard of Oz, and for that matter the entire "Oz" fantasy series, none of which happens to be banned? Based on these books — and children's reactions to them — the Religious Right's Thought Police should know that children are not going to begin praying to Satan and hope they can fly on a broomstick instead of riding the bus to school — even though the concept is an environmentally-friendly one — and that no amount of magic will enable a farmyard pig to converse with a spider.

But this logic isn't good enough for the Religious Right. They believe that Harry's adventures promote witchcraft, Satanism, and the recognition of supernatural powers other than the Almighty Bearded Christian God. True to form, they galvanize their troops in an attempt to get *"Harry Potter"* removed from schools, public libraries and condemned its sale at bookstores. And though some churches — such as the Harvest Assembly of God Church in Pennsylvania[62] and Christ Community Church in New Mexico[63] — have held book-burnings in Harry's name and some schools did remove *"Harry Potter"* from required course readings, the book was generally not banned and easily available to all who wanted it.

In fact, despite the onslaught of public fire-and-brimstone statements spewing from the Religious Right insisting that these books would lead children down the path of temptation and cause an unprecedented rise of eight year old Satan-worshippers offering sacrifices to the Evil One, the only behavioral change that could be seen in direct correlation to *"Harry Potter"* was that children were reading. In fact children were excited about reading, talking about what they had read, and wanted to read (and in some cases, write) more. A win-win on all fronts for parents, educators and children — but not, it seems, for the Religious Right's Thought Police.

As expected, and with delicious irony, the Religious Right's efforts to ban the book only fueled society's desire to read it, and almost doubled its sales. (Perhaps we should offer these "Family Values" groups up as sacrifice in the name of Sanity and Rationality. We'd probably be better off as a result.)

But the Religious Right's censorship efforts in entertainment are not limited to books — after all, *"Harry Potter"* aside, how many people in America read more than the daily comics in the newspaper?

In August 2002, the *Parents Television Council* (PTC) — another Religious Right group — decided to take on the highly acclaimed television series *Buffy The Vampire Slayer,* labeling it "the worst show in prime time."[64] Although a dark action-packed soap opera, it is one of the few shows on television that explores the teen angst years in a manner that not only doesn't insult the intelligence of its viewers but also shows teenagers — particularly girls — as competent and strong individuals in a male-dominated society.

Over the years, *Buffy* characters have accurately portrayed real-world issues important to their predominantly-teenaged viewers such as angst, disease, relationships, friendship, the death of a parent or loved one, sexual frustration and exploration, stress, lesbianism, the horrors of attempted rape, and even used an "addiction to magic" as the context for a well-written anti-drug message. The show doesn't talk down or preach to its audience but treats them as intelligent equals and allows them to interpret what they see however they wish.

Unfortunately, no matter how accurately *Buffy* reflects the trials and tribulations of real life for teens and adults (sans evil creatures of the night) it's still an evil program to the PTC, since the show refuses to accept and portray the dogmatic medieval view of Christian morality.

Here's a wake-up hymn, people: *Buffy* is entertainment, plain and simple, just like Harry Potter, Sabrina The Teenage Witch, Winnie The Pooh, Big Bird, and Wilbur The Talking Pig. Nothing more. If the program can help a person cope with the problems they're facing in their personal lives in a non-violent, non-destructive manner that looks out for their fellow humans, isn't that something the Religious Right's God would approve of? One would think so, but the PTC likely would disagree. Their version of the program would be *Buffy The Bible Reader*, whose gang smites Evil with good pronunciation and a Rosary. (You'd think they'd be happy that characters on the show used a cross to destroy evil, but no!)

To be truly enlightened, one needs to be exposed to *all* sides of an issue. This does not mean a person must agree with all sides or even with all arguments from any one side, but it's crucial to understand various perspectives on a given issue, even if it's an uncomfortable one. This is known as deductive reasoning and is the basis for many philosophies and the point of scholastic debate clubs. Without this ability, all a person has is knowledge without substance and an inculcated lack of tolerance based on limited information and a singular set of perceptions . . . and that's a breeding ground for the kinds of trouble that we currently see in many religious-based societies around the world.

Based on all this, I'd wager that this fact serves as the driving force behind the Religious Right and their Thought Police. These people are scared that children might learn that there are *other* spiritual or social paths besides the one they're promoting as absolute truth.

This is a normal reaction, I suppose, because it's clear that these groups are simply in the business of marketing a specific brand of God to the world, and, like any good business, they want to corner the market in its particular segment of the God industry.

It's a very competitive market, especially if your target audience is exposed to and willing to consider alternative products and vendors. And like any business trying to build a long-term and loyal customer base, they employ the effective marketing plan of "getting them while they're young."

I don't plan to impose my spiritual beliefs on anyone, particularly since I view spirituality as a deeply personal thing that varies from person to person. Morality isn't black-or-white, and sure isn't based on any one particular set of religious beliefs. To those who take pleasure in their self-serving mandate to impose their dogmatic beliefs on others, I tell them if their God doesn't like the way I live, or what I choose to read, watch, know, do, challenge, or acknowledge in this world, let *him* tell me, not you.

These organizations must have our Founding Fathers rolling in their graves wondering what they bothered to fight for when America was new.

Separation of church and state? Let's not kid ourselves.

14

America's Profitable Red Light Districts

In general the art of government consists in taking as much money as possible from one class of citizens to give to the other.
-Voltaire

Ever hear of Red Light Cameras? They may be coming to a city near you, but I'll wager you thought about something else when you saw the title of this essay — unless you're a member of the Religious Right, that is.

According to city officials and local lobby groups around the country, these devices are to reduce the potential for dangerous motorists running through intersections and helping to curb *"aggressive driving."* The system consists of a camera system that snaps photos of your vehicle as it cross an intersection after the light changes, which in turn makes you in immediate violation of local traffic laws. Some are relatively-obscure freestanding boxes on the sides of roads near intersections, while others are huge ugly glass domes hanging off of spidery arms across each lane of the street that visually-announce their Big Brother presence to all who drive under them.

Since in today's society, the computer never lies, and the camera provides a perfect record of the incident, *you're automatically guilty.* Gone is the chance to plead with the officer, there's no longer a chance to explain the situation that caused you to speed up; no chance of the officer issuing a warning or deciding after hearing your explanation to not give you a citation at all ... the cameras don't care. Their role is to serve as the unfeeling eyes of the city, enforcing whatever they're programmed to without prejudice, empathy, or realizing that no two situations are identical.

In other words, we're outsourcing this aspect of law enforcement. Get caught by the camera and you're guilty, guilty, *guilty until you can prove otherwise.*

Local municipalities love these things, and even the Federal Highway Administration (FHA) recognizes the benefits of red light cameras to local governments, going so far as to suggest that such problem intersections might serve as a great location to hold a press conference to espouse the need for red light camera systems.[65]

What we *aren't* told is that once the decision is made to deploy cameras, city officials almost always issue directives to shorten yellow light times. This means that when drivers come to an intersection with a shortened yellow time, they're faced with the choice either of stopping abruptly on yellow and risking a rear end accident — which according to any no-fault insurance policy and many state laws makes the driver equally liable for the accident — or accelerating and running the light, thus breaking the law and being cited by the camera and having points put on their license. Most drivers realize that either action is unsafe, yet the situation forces them to make a Catch-22 type decision nearly instantly. Is this dangerous? Certainly. At the very least, it's unsettling. All in all it's a lose-lose proposition for the driver.

On the other hand, this is a win-win situation for the local government because each time a driver faces this dilemma, governments increases its odds for hitting the jackpot by reaping free cash from speeding tickets ... and for each accident or red-light runner that it can add to the statistics, local governments can cite the need for even more cameras, and thus the clever revenue-collection cycle continues.

Of course, it's also a win-win situation for car insurance companies who get to raise their premiums for a whole new crop of "dangerous" drivers and rake in bigger profits.

So while it's unsettling and potentially dangerous for drivers, it's a cash cow for governments, their contractors, and the insurance industry.

For example, in 2000, a red light camera was installed at the intersection of Mission Bay Drive and Grand Avenue in San Diego. With its yellow-light time of 3 seconds the intersection produced about 2,300 violations every month.[66] The really ridiculous part is that it takes longer than the allotted three seconds of yellow to slow down from the posted speed limit when the driver first sees the light begin to change. Although dangerous, the 3 second yellow shows no signs of going away — not because it makes the community safer, but because it's just too damn profitable.

Each time someone ends up in an intersection on red in San Diego, the city collects a $271 fine, $70 of which is sent to the city's private contractor as fees for running and processing the camera system.[67] Thus, hefty traffic fines generated by mistimed traffic signals means big money for the cash-strapped city and more profit for the company running their traffic enforcement system.

To break it down into the simplest terms possible: a single camera managed to bring in $6.8 million just 18 months.[68] With that rate of return, it's no wonder these things are cropping up everywhere!

However, when the yellow light time for the above intersection was extended to 4.7 seconds as a test on July 28, 2000, red light violations *plummeted ninety percent*, and stayed there.[69] The simple (and inexpensive) task of adding a little over one second to the time the yellow light was illuminated produced a significant safety benefit for motorists by removing that forced Catch-22 decision and allowing them to slow down safely.

But did San Diego tell the world of its success, proclaiming that they managed to reduce the number of red light runners at their intersections and increase both driver and pedestrian safety? Did it move to correct signal timing at other intersections? The answer is obvious — of course it didn't, as doing so would eat into their profits and that of the auto insurance industry when fender-benders occur as a driver tries to comply with finagled traffic signals and avoid a ticket.

Likewise, Washington, D.C., installed red light cameras in 2001 with the declared goal of improving road safety by "calming roads" in and around the nation's capitol. Yet in late 2002, faced with a city budget deficit of over $200 million, Mayor Anthony Williams announced that the city was going to vigorously expand its use of red light cameras because "the city needs the money."[70]

While Mayor Williams had the decency to be honest, it goes without saying that like many other government projects involving private contractors, red light cameras are popping up faster than you say "conflict-of-interest."

In San Diego, if a driver challenges a red light citation, not only must they pay in advance before getting their hearing with a city hearing officer or traffic judge, but the judge can only make recommendations back to the camera company on whether or not they think the driver was liable for the citation. It is now up to the red light camera manufacturer to decide whether to refund the money or not. As a publicly traded business with an eye on profit and shareholder return, how many of these citations do you think Lockheed Martin is going to refund? After all, the goal of business is to make money, not give it back!

Who's really enforcing traffic laws, and when did Lockheed Martin become an arm of the judicial branch? Not to mention, such systems are prone to abuse.

In 2001, San Diego police had to audit all their cameras when they discovered that Lockheed Martin — the private defense contractor operating their red light cameras – relocated the underground sensors that activate the cameras at three intersections.[71] Was Lockheed Martin simply trying to improve the accuracy of the cameras, or was this an attempt to generate more citations and profit by taking advantage of unwitting drivers and city employees?

Remember speed traps? Red light cameras now serve as a new-and-improved version of that age-old revenue-generating scam. For example, in some small Texas towns, ridiculously low speed limits were set for major roads and interstates but motorists remained largely unaware, since the towns "accidentally" allowed trees and shrubs to partially obscure the posted speed limit signs. Local judges would counter this defense by drivers in traffic court, citing that "ignorance of the law is no excuse." As a result of public protest over these shady municipal revenue-generating techniques, the Texas legislature passed an annual cap on the amount of revenue any municipality could claim from speeding violations on state or federal roadways within the state.[72] As expected, the practice abruptly declined, indicating unequivocally that *public safety played no part* in the decision to deploy the red light cameras.

Consider that the Institute of Transportation Engineers is actively involved in lobbying for, and even drafting legislation to, implement red light cameras. The group is closely tied to the Insurance Institute for Highway Safety (IIHS), an entity funded by companies that stand to profit every time points are assessed to a driver's license.[73]

The FHA even provides checklists for local officials to use when calling for the installation of additional red light cameras and touting their alleged safety benefits[74] — and, of course, no mention is made about the revenue benefits for the city. It's assumed they hope funds received from red light cameras will go into local road safety programs, but we all know better. It's an established truism that free money never goes where it's needed most.

It seems the only documented benefit to red light cameras is to the organizations that install and administer them, as they convert traffic law enforcement into a business practice with the ultimate goal of turning millions of unwitting drivers into a nearly limitless source of free revenue.

I guess such practices are good for business, and that's good for America.

15

Homeland Insecurity

Patrick Henry never said, 'Give me absolute safety or give me death!'
- John Stossel

Perhaps the terrorists are winning, and we're just too caught up in our own Star-Spangled American egos to admit it. After all, the stated goal of the September 11 terrorists and their leader was to "destroy" America by attacking those things that mattered most to our society.

Only an idiot would think that simply meant iconic buildings or people.

Sure, that sort of destruction causes damage and chaos, but you can always rebuild buildings, and you can generally make more people. Of course, both efforts require time, money, and effort, but they can be done.

As we move through 2003 and the second year of The New Normal, I join with those who — contrary to the sentiment of our national leaders and much-ballyhooed innovations like the National Terror Alert Color System and introduction of "Gate-Rape" to the lexicon of American air travel — quietly believe the terrorists have already won.

And they did it with the full cooperation of the United States Government.

In no place is this more prominently proven than at America's airports, the epitome of America's New Normal, where everyone is presumed guilty until proven guiltier.

It used to be that air travel was annoying. Now, it's invasive, embarrassing, confusing, and more annoying than ever. And despite a time of severe financial belt-tightening, people are choosing to pay a premium to fly non-stop just to avoid the risk of a delay if the terminal they use during a layover is evacuated after someone finds tweezers — no doubt missed by a screener and having nothing to do with terrorism — in the garbage.

Of course, that might not happen if screeners managed to keep their new security equipment plugged in and functioning in the first place[75] or if the new federal airport screeners could stay awake at their posts, the latter causing the near-total evacuation of Seattle-Tacoma Airport in January 2003.[76]

To his credit, and to partially accommodate the needs of customer service with security, the new Director of the Transportation Security Agency (TSA) James Loy won the hearts and minds of America's traveling public — when, in late 2002, he proclaimed that drinks in paper or foam cups could be carried through metal detectors at security checkpoints.[77] Still no can is allowed, however — even if you swill from it as you go through security.

However, cans or not, we can also thank him for eliminating the stupid questions — such as "has anyone unknown to you asked you to carry anything onboard?" — routinely asked at check-in counters.[78] I guess that after fourteen years, the government finally realizes that security experts were correct — if a terrorist intends to blow himself up, the criminal penalties for lying to a ticket agent aren't going to be much of a deterrent.

But it's not all for the better. Going into the 2002 Christmas holidays, TSA asked travelers *not* to lock their suitcases sent through as checked baggage — you know, the stuff riding under the plane that we can't get to until after we land.[79] This was to make it easier for the newly federalized baggage screeners to conduct security inspections of checked baggage. Yet it seems nobody at TSA considered how much easier this policy makes it for unscrupulous airline baggage handlers to steal things — something we hear about in the news every few months.

TSA even ran diagrams in major newspapers showing passengers how to pack their suitcases to facilitate security screening of their checked baggage. Or, more accurately, where to put the things a potential thief should ignore when rummaging through your luggage looking for loot as your Samsonite gets sent to your airplane.

The only hope left is that FEDEX begins offering consumer-friendly rates to anyone with proof of an airline ticket purchase so that we can ship our belongings in advance of our travel and avoid the whole checked-baggage fiasco. Better yet, FEDEX could create people-sized cartons so that we could overnight-ship ourselves to our destination. All an individual would need to do is bring his or her own food, water, and reading material for the flight — which shouldn't be a major inconvenience, as most airline passengers have grown accustomed to fending for themselves with the cutbacks in passenger service over the years anyway.

Then there's the wonderful experience passengers have flying into and out of the Washington, D.C. area through Reagan National Airport. For the first 30 minutes on all outbound flights, and the last 30 minutes on all inbound flights, passengers are prohibited from standing or moving around the cabin.[80] Need to use the restroom? Regardless if you're aged eight or eighty, you better hold it, cross your legs, or invest in some TSA-approved adult diapers, because if you're seen standing during this time, you're liable to be arrested and detained as a potential terrorist.

And of course, anything made of metal larger than a key still is subject to confiscation by the newly uniformed and federalized TSA Airport Security Screeners — as if *Death by Tweezers* was ever something the traveling public was worried about. Nobody seems to mention that September 11 was attributed in large part to easily forced cockpit doors and *not* the presence of sharp objects in the hands of passengers. The terrorists could have commandeered the planes with a plastic spoon and the right amount of yelling if they wanted to. But, to reassure the public and present an image of higher security at airports, anything that might be — or possibly looks — dangerous is confiscated. It's like those sponge NERF footballs you buy at *Toys 'R Us* — you know, the things that look and throw like a real football, but have little real potential for injury when you're hit with one.

Even wearing an underwire bra – which sets off the detectors now — cause women passengers to be searched more closely at checkpoints. These women are directed to one side and searched quite closely by TSA screeners — and modesty isn't a concern in the face of safety either. Pregnant, and naturally a tad self-conscious about your figure? Or perhaps carrying a kinky sex toy in your tote bag? Your modesty is not a concern to the United States of America — just raise your arms, drop your pants, and try not to cry in embarrassment as onlookers gawk as each panty, bra, sock, and tampon is held up in the air for TSA – and public - inspection.

Somehow I don't think underwire bras, panties, or tampons are a national security threat, nor should people be forced to spend time thinking about what to wear before flying. Comedian Dennis Miller once ranted that mandating hospital scrubs and paper booties might not be a far-fetched idea given how goofy airport security's become these days — and in the face of the ever growing humiliations, he just might have been onto something.

I'm waiting for TSA rules to require all passengers don straitjackets and be administered a shot or two of Demerol before boarding the aircraft. And perhaps, to offset the exorbitant costs necessary to improve America's airport security, TSA could install video cameras at security checkpoints and charge $20 an hour for Internet users around the world to see real-time color videos of passengers being strip-searched, scanned, fondled, and groped (in other words, "gate-raped") at our airports.

Soft-core porn from hard-core security — what a concept! (Patent Pending.)

Of course, all this is done to assure the public that Uncle Sam is doing everything in its power to prevent another September 11-type of attack. That's to be expected, but it'd be appreciated more if the security measures implemented were really effective and not just a public relations ploy to cajole folks back into the air by presenting an image of strong security. After all, while the average person found it impressive, most of the National Guard troops posted at airports following September 11 didn't have ammunition for their weapons — and some didn't even have weapons!

Despite all of the new airline security rules, regulations and overhauls, I believe that the single best improvement to the safety of our air travel system were the heroics of the crew and passengers on United Flight 93 over Pennsylvania on September 11. The old standing rule about cooperating with hijackers is now obsolete; today's passengers just won't allow another commercial airliner to be hijacked — or turned into a guided weapon — without a fight, regardless of how the bad guys are armed. It's the new "Let's Roll" defense, and as we saw on September 11, it worked perfectly over Pennsylvania.

But these new security procedures don't operate in a vacuum. Sure, they're designed to screen everyone boarding an aircraft, but what about those who the government really thinks are *potential* evildoers?

After September 11, the FBI began to circulate its closely held Potential Terrorist Watch List to other government and private sector entities under the codename PROJECT LOOKOUT — an unprecedented move for an agency hell-bent on maintaining secrets at all costs given its links to the intelligence community. As a December 2002 *Wall Street Journal* article noted:

> Departing from its usual practice of closely guarding such lists, the FBI circulated the names of hundreds of people it wanted to question. Counter-terrorism officials gave the list to car-rental companies. Then FBI field agents and other officials circulated it to big banks, travel-reservations systems, firms that collect consumer data, as well as casino operators such as MGM Mirage, the owner of 'New York-New York.' Additional recipients included businesses thought vulnerable to terrorist intrusion, including truckers, chemical companies and power-plant operators. It was the largest intelligence-sharing experiment the bureau has ever undertaken with the private sector.
>
> A year later, the list has taken on a life of its own, with multiplying — and error-filled — versions being passed around like bootleg music. Some companies fed a version of the list into their own databases and now use it to screen job applicants and customers... the watch list shared with companies — one part of the FBI's massive counter-terrorism database — quickly became obsolete as the bureau worked its way through the names. The FBI's counter-terrorism division quietly stopped updating the list more than a year ago. But it never informed most of the companies that had received a copy. FBI headquarters doesn't know who is still using the list because officials never kept track of who got it.[81]

Naturally, there are numerous reports of innocent citizens being wrongfully surveilled and reported to the FBI as potential terrorists because their names still appeared on a Watch List after the FBI had deemed them not a threat and removed them from newer lists. One wonders what the criterion is to get on — or off — that list. From what I hear, it's like the Hotel California – you can check out, but you can never leave.

And if that's not bad enough, the Pentagon tapped retired Admiral (and pardoned Iran-Contra felon) John Poindexter to head up a new Orwellian Big Brother project innocuously-dubbed "Total Information Awareness" (TIA). The project — funded from the Pentagon but not directly authorized by Congress — seeks to monitor the activities and interests of everyone inside the United States, including all citizens and visitors.

As *New York Times* columnist William Safire wrote in late 2002 about TIA:

> Every prescription you buy and medical prescription you fill, every Web site you visit and e-mail you send or receive, every academic grade you receive, every bank deposit you make, every trip you book and every event you attend — all these transactions and communications will go into what the Defense Department describes as "a virtual, centralized grand database."
>
> To this computerized dossier on your private life from commercial sources, add every piece of information that government has about you — passport application, driver's license and bridge toll records, judicial and divorce records, complaints from nosy neighbors to the F.B.I., your lifetime paper trail plus the latest hidden camera surveillance — and you have the supersnoop's dream: a "Total Information Awareness" about every U.S. citizen.[82]

The goal of TIA is to create a "normal" profile for each American and then use its systems to search for any irregularities — such as a computer geek (like me) suddenly purchasing books on terrorism or bio-warfare or a person who never flies suddenly traveling one-way across the country — and then alerting law enforcement about this "potential terrorist." One wonders how Poindexter's team would react if a college film major decided to switch majors to chemistry or physics without advance warning.

In keeping with the Bush administration's (questionable) foreign policies, TIA seeks to prevent future terrorism by doing anything it possibly can to pre-empt it. As mentioned elsewhere in this book, TIA is a federal initiative eerily similar to the concept of "Pre-Crime" portrayed in Steven Spielberg's 2002 blockbuster movie, *Minority Report."* Nothing is too outrageous in the fight against terrorism: another of Poindexter's research projects tries to detect terrorists by their "gait" – how a person walks - and then use public surveillance cameras to scan for bad guys.

Interestingly, as the public controversy over TIA grew toward the end of 2002, the TIA website began to shrink as increasing amounts of information — such as the names and biographies of its staff — were removed from public access on the Internet. Of course, this only increased the controversy surrounding the project and does nothing to increase public (or Congressional) trust and support for the venture.

As a result of public and Congressional outcry, in mid-2003, TIA was renamed to *"Terrorist* Information Awareness" in a lame effort to allay fears of a Pentagon-operated Big Brother monitoring every law-abiding American's activities. The goal and motive of the program remains the same, despite the more patriotic-sounding, Homeland Security-oriented moniker, and the protests still continue on this very controversial program.

TIA is one of the many post-September-11 programs intending to "Secure the Homeland" from *anything* remotely evil. We've already heard that the FBI is visiting libraries to see if anyone's checked out anything deemed "suspicious" and that new federal laws prevent librarians from disclosing that the FBI was ever there. It's turning out that librarians and booksellers are the new front-line shock troops in the vaunted War on Terror, defending America right alongside college registrars and diving- or flight-school owners. In the case of libraries, Assistant Attorney General Daniel Bryant believes that "Americans who borrow or buy books surrender their right of privacy."[83]

If that isn't a draconian, Big Brother, un-American incursion into the legal activities and privacy of law-abiding American citizens, I don't know what is. It makes you wonder if in the future anyone caught purchasing — or thinking about trying — a different brand of toothpaste than the Attorney General uses will become a "person of interest" to the FBI. Perhaps even by purchasing and reading this book, you're now on a government watch list. Talk about fostering a climate of thought control and laying the foundation for a police state.

Of course, the librarians,[84] shop owners, and trade associations challenging this sudden, secretive shift in the presumption of guilt and invasion of privacy were attacked publicly as being "unpatriotic" in the government's efforts in the war against terrorism.

More frighteningly, law-abiding Americans don't know if they're being targeted as a potential terrorist because there's no accountability or oversight on how Terrorist Watch Lists are developed, distributed, or updated. There is also no way to know whether a person's normal law-abiding activities will be deemed "suspicious" according to some secret and vague set of terrorist-spotting government guidelines — and, like our credit reports, it's nearly impossible to change your records when there's a mistake.

For instance, in December 2002, Ralph Omholt — a US citizen and experienced pilot licensed to fly the Boeing 737 — purchased a commercial CD-ROM-based training program on how to fly the 737 from a seller on Internet auction site eBay. Soon after he received the item, the panicked seller contacted him and said he needed the CD-ROM back — promising a full refund — because the FBI had learned about the auction and said the information on the CD-ROM constituted a "national security threat."

Omholt received a grand jury subpoena for a terror-related investigation on December 17. In an article about his situation published the day before his subpoena arrived (once someone receives a subpoena served under the USA PATRIOT Act they're not allowed to tell anyone about it) Omholt wondered if realistic computer simulation games like Microsoft Flight Simulator would be changed, licensed, or deemed a "national security threat" because of their contents. He said:

> There are more than 66,000 airline pilots and about 650,000 private pilots in the United States today, according to aviation industry records. What the members of this vast and diverse group have in common is: *They are continuously training and rehearsing their flight skills, a task that requires access to flight instructional material such as the 'suddenly dangerous' B-737 CD-ROM disk that had fallen into my possession.*[85]

When are we going to recognize and acknowledge the sheer absurdity of what's happening in our nation's airports and around the country in the name of security? Ask any legitimate security expert: it's impossible to enact total security, particularly in a society and culture that cherishes freedom of movement and expression.

Only an idiot would assume it's possible to achieve total security, yet we've given up our liberties for no demonstrable increase in safety by throwing all logic to the wind and simply accepting what we're asked to accept by our confused federal government as it tries to respond to emerging national security challenges.

As this book went to press, the Pentagon was looking to award a contract to develop what it calls "Combat Zones that Can See" – using thousands of remote cameras to read license plates, scan faces, and track the movement of a person or vehicle anywhere it travels in a city. Despite the Pentagon's claims this technology would be used "according to federal law" (something that can change rather easily) and primarily overseas, it's only a matter of time before state and local law enforcement – or the new Homeland Security Department – tries to use this type of Big Brother surveillance in American cities, most likely under the guise of "protecting the Homeland."

Naturally, American citizens and travelers — pardon me, victims — have little option but to cooperate fully and quietly with post-September-11 searches, surveillance, and requirements or risk being arrested and forever marked as a potential Enemy of the State. And, if your name does appear on such a list, consider yourself an American outcast in the eyes of Uncle Sam, *even if you're completely innocent*...and be prepared for any number of government-imposed inconveniences as you live, work, and travel around the United States, since it's going to be next to impossible to get your name off such watch lists. You're guilty until proven guiltier; the new American legal standard.

Display hesitation, grumble, or question some new, perhaps strange security policy and you're begging for trouble under the Catch-22 belief that if you're not guilty, you won't mind these intrusions. And, given the level of ignorance and complacency in our society today, folks will just shuffle through checkpoints and do whatever's asked of them, because they don't have the intelligence to recognize this lunacy for what it really is. Besides, if you are a thinking person, have some modicum of common sense, and do question something, you might be labeled a "person of interest" to federal law enforcement.

Must our cherished American liberties be destroyed in order to save them?

James Madison, one of America's prominent Founding Fathers, wrote that, "perhaps it is a universal truth that the loss of liberty at home is to be charged to provisions against danger, real or pretended, from abroad."

He was right — since September 11, not only are we *not* safer from foreign terrorists, but being terrified by our own government as well.

16

The Terror Alert They Won't Issue

The whole aim of practical politics is to keep the populace alarmed (and hence clamorous to be led to safety) by menacing it with an endless series of hobgoblins, all of them imaginary.
- H. L. Mencken

Let's face it; America in 2003 is one confused nation.

Granted, we've always been confused about some things — the metric system, what ABC was thinking when they picked their fall lineup (again), do the girls in the *"Gone Wild"* series *really* strip for just anyone, and does Pepsi or Coke taste better with rum, to name a few befuddling questions debated in our society these days — but it seems that nearly everyone can agree that they are confused with how to continue living their daily lives in the new Age of Terror in America.

Since September 11, 2001, the repeated message of the federal government to the American citizen is to *"continue living your lives normally"* while continuing to *"be on alert"* for anything *"out of the ordinary"* that might indicate a potential terrorist act in the making.

This may sound meaningful and can even be spun as necessary in our collective post-September-11 consciousness, but let's be totally honest: it's hard to live a normal life when being inundated with vaguely-worded predictions of doom and gloom. Over and over we're warned that anything, anywhere — from shopping malls to the Statue of Liberty — is now a potential target, but yet we should go about our lives as though everything were normal despite the rotating National Terror Alert Colors floating across our TV screens and the incessant reports of alleged terror cells and potential terror plots being broken up daily in our home towns.

Talk about a mixed message that creates a national psychosis, especially given the relative lack of common sense and collective ignorance shown by many Americans these days that's been mentioned elsewhere in this book.

As if that wasn't overkill enough, the Partnership for Public Warning even suggested creating a Terror Beeper system to transmit alerts about potential terror attacks or changes to America's Terror Alert Condition to Americans on their cell phones and pagers — whether they want to receive them or not — and designing consumer television sets to automatically turn themselves on when a Terror Alert is issued.[86]

Hello, Mister President! We *know* we've been attacked, and we know that there's a chance of future successful attacks in our country despite the best efforts of the government to protect us. Like it or not, it's a fact of life that we have been forced to accept. It may come as a surprise that Americans are a hardy bunch — maybe we're a bit confused at times, but we're not complete dummies. All these breathless warnings, analysis, alert reports and spinning security color schemes do is perpetuate a culture of national fear and bankrupt our state and local emergency services agencies. And, I'm not going to appreciate being inundated by Homeland Security alert faxes, e-mail, or text messages whenever Dick Cheney gets indigestion.

That being said, let's reflect on some of what America was warned about "might happen soon" during one four-day period in 2002:

- May 20: Defense Secretary Rumsfeld tells Senators that terrorists will eventually obtain weapons of mass destruction.

- May 20: FBI Director Mueller says that Palestinian-style suicide bombings on US soil is "inevitable."

- May 21: The FBI reports "possible terrorist threat" to US oil facilities.

- May 21: President Bush echoes Rumsfeld's warning about terrorists obtaining weapons of mass destruction.

- May 21: The FBI warns of potential attacks against major landmarks in the US, particularly in New York City.

- May 21: The FBI circulates warning to apartment and condominium owners of possible terrorist activity in their buildings.

- May 22: US Government warns its citizens in the Arab world against possible terror attacks.

- May 24: US Transportation Department issues warning over possible terror attacks on transit, rail, and subway systems.

- May 24: The Nuclear Regulatory Commission warns 103 US nuclear plants of "possible terrorist attacks" (by small planes) and to "be alert."

- May 24: The FBI warns that terrorists may develop an "offensive scuba diver capability" to conduct attacks.

Several people I spoke with in Washington, DC shook their heads in disbelief that the government went public over the actual possibility of "terrorist scuba divers" — especially since the FBI alert stated *"while there is no evidence of operational planning to utilize scuba divers to carry out attacks within the United States, there is a body of information showing the desire to obtain such capability* [to attack the United States.]"

The fact is that terrorists may indeed employ scuba divers, but they could just as easily employ parachutists, schoolteachers, bus drivers, or hunting-school owners. Scarier yet, they could employ people who have no idea that they've been employed. This has been known to happen with spectacular results; in fact it happened some years back to a very nice, very pregnant, very "non-profile-able" German woman whose Palestinian boyfriend packed her suitcase (and placed inside a bomb she didn't know about) before she boarded an El Al flight to Tel Aviv. Should every individual you see on the street generate potential terror alerts? We're heading in that direction.

If anything, the events of September 11 should be understood as a significant and *already-demonstrated desire and capability* by certain fundamentalist entities to attack Americans either in the United States or across the globe by whatever means necessary or available. This could include use of crop dusters, kamikaze pilots, hot air balloons, trains, trucks, and weapons of mass destruction.

It probably includes offensive scuba divers, too.

Unfortunately this warning is typical, and getting more typical as we move into 2003. The Federal Government is displaying a slightly schizophrenic pattern of behavior, issuing warnings and then backtracking, if not retracting them — quite clearly indicating to the world that no matter what the media is reporting, or the powerful rhetoric coming from Washington, the federal government is still confused about how to deal with terrorism effectively.

This confusion trickles down to the states and cities in America that are forced to spend millions of dollars for overtime and extra resources each time the national alert status is raised and they should "be on guard" for the increased *possibility* of a terrorist attack; obviously this isn't a popular course of action given the serious financial difficulties many states are experiencing these days. As a result, some states have told the Homeland Security Department that they're going to ignore any increases in the Homeland Alert Color Status unless it directly relates to their state – it just costs too much, and they simply can't afford it. Besides, the current terror alerts are too general in nature, and not every state, city, or county has an equal likelihood for attack.

Of course, this confusion also impacts on the average rank-and-file citizen. In February 2003, just as America went on Orange Alert (the second-highest terror alert) the newly-minted Homeland Security Department caused a national panic when it suggested that citizens purchase extra food and supplies and use duct tape and plastic sheeting to seal up their homes in the event of a terrorist attack.[87] Citizens flocked to supermarkets and hardware stores in a national frenzy not seen since the "Duck and Cover" days of the Cold War.

Despite the rush to hardware stores, few people wondered what they would do after the air ran out in their duct-tape sealed rooms while they were still inside. (Some analysts argue that would help reduce the numbers of clueless idiots in America, and thus provide a beneficial side-effect.) That same week, it was learned that the intelligence source that led to the Duct Tape Orange Alert was deemed unreliable by intelligence analysts, having failed a polygraph test after his information was passed to the Homeland Security Department – and acted upon - as "credible."

At this point, the only people benefiting from America's scatterbrained domestic response to terrorism are the nations that have lived for decades with a constant threat of terrorism — such as Israel, the United Kingdom and Ireland – whose comedians are being provided an endless amount of material to work with as America struggles to deal effectively with the problems of terrorism.

Therefore, as a public service, I offer this Standard Terror Warning (copyright pending) — a simple statement intended to clarify the reality of America's Homeland Security alert status and make it easier for us to move ahead with our lives in the post-9/11 reality, just as other nations have for decades:

> *** Standard Terror Warning ***
>
> Based on past actions, it is quite likely that terrorists will attempt to attack the United States in the future. However, we are unsure when, where, or how this may occur, given the unconventional nature of terrorism and the nearly-countless ways in which such entities may conduct their attacks.
>
> It should be noted that America is not alone in this unfortunate situation — nations such as the United Kingdom, Germany, Israel, France and Italy have continued to maintain productive and relatively peaceful societies despite similar conditions and extensive terror-related kidnappings and bombings over several decades.
>
> Given that America is no longer immune from acts of foreign terror within its borders, citizens and authorized foreign visitors to the United States are advised that they can either spend their lives cowering in fear, hiding in their basements, or continue to live out their lives, understanding that America — despite all it offers — has changed slightly for the worse, whether they like it or not.
>
> *** Standard Terror Warning ***

The harsh reality is that American culture has been forever changed; but nobody in charge wants to come out and admit it publicly. And that's the wrong approach.

The public is better served by a simple official acknowledgement of the new American Reality. Despite the ever-increasing Homeland Security laws, federalized security jobs, runaway funding, and media spin about how America "hasn't changed," it has. The truth is that the United States will continue to be an enticing target for its enemies, and as a result, there's an unfortunate and tragic likelihood of future attacks on our soil by a variety of means and methods.

Tiptoeing around the reality of the situation and bombarding the public with vague warnings of little value doesn't help the American war effort, raise morale, or reassure our citizens. Ironically, these warnings only force us to look over our shoulders and shiver in fear, creating a culture of national paranoia and confusion in our once-free society, something the terrorists probably wanted to accomplish all along.

Plato believed that no law or ordinance is mightier than understanding. It's time to come clean and accept our current reality. Americans, for all our shortcomings, can understand the truth. We may not like it, but we can — and must — accept it.

17

The New Normal

Patriotic societies seem to think that the way to educate school children in a democracy is to stage bigger and better flag saluting.
- S.I. Hayakawa

By now, it should be obvious that while the American people are fickle about whether they would rather "have a Coke and a smile" or be part of "the Pepsi generation," and they may agree to disagree about which TV doctor gives better advice for relieving anxiety, ever since the events of September 11 they tend to leap with a herd-like, almost faith-based mentality on matters of vital interest and national policy.

Ask for an opinion from any random person on the street pertaining to a policy currently in debate in Congress or on the news (er, "info-tainment") channels, and you'll hear that the president is correct — not that they will know what was said, they'll simply say, "the President is correct." Worse yet, they'll simply echo whatever they heard on the television, but be unable to form their own opinion on the matter being discussed.

While America once cherished freedom of speech as a basic inalienable right and prided itself on allowing all law-abiding citizens and visitors to participate in peaceful dissent to promote public debate and education on critical policy matters, things have changed for the worse.

While this has been a growing problem for some time, particularly since September 2001, the American public seems perfectly content to unquestioningly support, rubber stamp, and participate in anything proposed by the president or his advisors, no matter how strange, far-reaching, or contrary to American ideals and the basic tenants of our Constitution it may be. This is facilitated by the previously mentioned overall lack of education and public awareness demonstrated by the average American citizen.

As already mentioned, this groupthink is especially disheartening to anyone wishing to express a loyally-dissenting opinion as is their right as Americans — they will be condemned in the strongest possible terms by everyone from their neighbor to the president himself.

Therefore, as a patriotic American, I offer the following analysis of America's New Normal, drawn from an anonymous e-mail sent to me in early 2002 as America was still recovering from the September 2001 attacks on its soil.

After all, as President Theodore Roosevelt said back in 1918, "To announce that there must be no criticism of the president, or that we are to stand by the president right or wrong, is not only unpatriotic and servile, but is morally treasonable to the American public."

Since I'm no traitor and love my country, I'm comfortable — if not a bit disturbed — to report that since September 11, it seems people are:

- *Normal* if you think suddenly buying a flag makes you patriotic; *abnormal* if you think suddenly buying and displaying a flag, without respecting and honoring the principles it represents, is a meaningless gesture, done only to conform to the groupthink of society around you.

- *Normal* if you think the best way to be patriotic is to "go out and buy something"; *abnormal* if you think patriotism and capitalism are separate entities.

- *Normal* if you think every national leader appearing in public must wear an American flag on their lapel to show national spirit; *abnormal* if you think the last time so many national leaders wore flags on their lapels was in the Soviet Politburo during the Cold War.

- *Normal* if you think the "War on Terror" is every bit as effective as we're told; *abnormal* if you question why, despite the billions spent on the "War on Terror" so far, we've been unable to locate our two favorite targets - Osama bin Laden or Saddam Hussein. – and bring them to justice, whatever that might be.

- *Normal* if you suddenly think George W. Bush is a good leader; *abnormal* if you think that terrorist attacks don't make anyone a good leader overnight, and would like to see more effective policy enacted and fewer meaningless sound bytes and axioms.

- *Normal* if you feel it's unpatriotic to peacefully and publicly criticize political leadership and policies during war; *abnormal* if you feel justified to question things that seem strange, always, regardless of circumstance, and think that this is the best way to be patriotic, especially in a nation that cherishes freedom, liberty, and tolerance.

- *Normal* if you feel the terrorist acts "puts things in perspective"; *abnormal* if you feel that the only thing that needs to be put in perspective is the self-importance America seems to place on itself above others in the world.

- *Normal* if you think airport security needs to be increased; *abnormal* if you think airport security, or any security, won't stop evil and psychotic people from committing evil and psychotic acts of violence and murder. You are even *more* abnormal if you question most security changes made at American airports because they don't seem to really be effective security measures at all.

- *Normal* if you think technology, such as biometrics, thumbprint scanners, and government ID cards will improve security; *abnormal* if you think technology can also thwart "improved security," and that the people advocating technological solutions are those who can profit from them.

- *Normal* if you think now is a time to embrace religion and be thankful; *abnormal* if you think religion and the shameless promotion of the "American God" of Christianity does more harm than good.

- *Normal* if you think it's acceptable to create a new organization to provide intelligence analysis that conveniently supports the Administration's stated political goals prior to war; *abnormal* if you believe that effective and objective intelligence analysis is best left to those specialists in the intelligence community who know and care much more about the subject they're examining than domestic politics.

- *Normal* if you think America's cherished civil liberties can be pushed aside in times of crisis and war, "for the good of America"; *abnormal* if you think America's constitutional rights are more important than any war or response to aggression, and government efforts to permanently remove or sidestep them means the enemy wins.

- *Normal* if you think freedoms — movement, speech, forming opinions, and others — should be lessened for improved safety, and that there isn't a 'civil liberties struggle' in America right now; *abnormal* if you think one hundred percent safety is not achievable, all future terrorist attacks cannot be prevented, and that such restrictions on freedom don't do anything useful except provide others with the ability to control you and the terrorists to gloat in victory.

- *Normal* if you think declaring "war" on terrorism will make it go away; *abnormal* if you think that declaring war on something, especially non-geographical entities, such as terrorism, drugs, poverty, AIDS, file-sharing, to name but a few of our current "wars," will not cause that thing to go away, but rather is a term used for public relations and building a new government bureaucracy.

- *Normal* if you think it is unpatriotic to politely disagree if you feel like it and not go along with the crowd; and *abnormal* if you think sheep are stupid animals, and in light of recent events, so are many Americans.

18

Greed Respects No Tragedy

You are not what you own.
- Rock band Fugazi

Want to know how money corrupts? Or, more exactly, how greedy and self-serving some Americans can be during times of national crisis? Let's look at a few disturbing examples.

In the aftermath of the 2001 World Trade Center attack, the federal government established a Victims' Compensation Fund to help the survivors of those killed on September 11. Through various calculations, averages, and predictions, the fund would pay an equitable amount to each survivor's family.

Believe it or not, one year after the attack, it was reported that brokerage firm Cantor Fitzgerald, one of the financial companies in the World Trade Center, filed a statement with the Justice Department regarding the Fund. The firm argued that the families of their high-income earners — some of whom made more than the projected $1.5 million award — should be eligible for considerably higher benefits (read "more free cash") from the fund than the families of other victims making less.[88]

What Cantor Fitzgerald essentially said was that in its eyes someone whose business card reads "Vice President of Investments" is worth more than someone who is responsible for cleaning the executive washroom floor, refilling coffee urns, or transferring client calls to an executive's cellular phone that's moving between the sixteenth and seventeenth holes on the golf course when it finally rings.

What an appalling sense of values and a pathetic example of human greed.

Think about it — if you've got $10 million or more in the family bank accounts and rake in $3 million or so a year in salary, bonus, and commissions, you're not going to be relocating from your Westchester mansion, selling your Lexus SUV, and moving to a homeless shelter anytime soon. Granted, the loss of a family member is always tragic, but your lifestyle probably won't change that much for the worse. Just cut back on the Omaha Steaks, DVDs, designer fashions, and country club memberships, and you'll still be able to send the kids to college.

But if you've got $20,000 or less in the bank, only take home $40,000 - $60,000 or so a year in salary and bonuses, and have to make payments on your modest rented apartment or small house with a hefty mortgage, you're probably going to be impacted much more quickly than your Saville Row wearing counterparts who don't rely on mass transit to get to work.

Those fighting for increased survivor benefits for Cantor's big-earners forget that the only reason these executives made the money they did was because their underlings and minions — making considerably less than they did — did their jobs so well. In case it needs to be remembered that top earners don't become top earners on their own.

Who's really hurting here?

Then there's Denise Lyman, the New York City landlord demanding (at last count) nearly $30,000 from the estate of 29 year-old September 11 victim Danielle Kousoulis who died within days of signing a new lease on her Upper West Side apartment. Lyman went so far as to move her family into Kousoulis' apartment and according to CBS News, took steps to prevent the victim's family or the Salvation Army from entering and clearing the apartment because, in her eyes, Kousoulis terminated her lease early (by being killed in the attack) and thus according to the lease, her estate was responsible for paying the rent.[89]

It's only fair — and besides, it's business.

Of course, we can't forget the phrase "Let's Roll" — uttered by United Flight 93 passenger Todd Beamer over his cell phone call to his wife before leading a group of passengers to re-take control of the hijacked jetliner over Pennsylvania. These two words became a national catch phrase in the weeks following September 11, and began showing up t-shirts, hats, and posters, even used by the President during his 2002 State of the Union address.

At last count, there are over a dozen entities seeking US trademark protection for the phrase.[90] It seems that this heroic phrase is too good to pass up trying to profit from; it's truly the gift that keeps on giving.

One wonders if Eleanor Roosevelt thought about trademarking the term "Day of Infamy" used by her husband in the years following the Pearl Harbor attack.

You'd think people would have a sense of human decency and a shred of compassion about the victims of such horrific events as the attacks of September 11. Bend a few rules and perhaps change the way business is done for a little while, as we realize that for a brief, tragic, moment, all victims and survivors of such a tragedy are equals.

Instead, despite the patriotic flag-waving and heated desire for retribution, we see people and companies using the tragedy as just another springboard to exploit and profit from, for no other reason than because they're too shallow to feel — or know — any differently.

Shame on them all.

19

The Approaching Digital Dark Ages

Technology is a queer thing. It brings you great gifts with one hand, and it stabs you in the back with the other.
— C. P. Snow

In a 1970 essay, author Lewis Mumford wrote about a "technological compulsiveness" developing in Western society, pointing out that the West:

> Accepted as unquestionable a technological imperative that is quite as arbitrary as the most primitive taboo: not merely is it the duty to foster invention and constantly to create technological novelties, but [it is] equally the duty to surrender to these novelties unconditionally just because they are offered, without respect to their human consequences.[91]

In the decades since that article appeared, the Western world has not only proven the validity of Mumford's observations, but it has taken its obsession with staying on the technological cutting-edge to levels he may never have imagined, especially in terms of consumer consumables such as cars, home theaters, cellular phones, and computers. With each new model year or partial increase in power or features, owners of existing products — even those from less than a year ago — become embittered as they begin to perceive themselves as second-class citizens and their desire to upgrade renews itself.

Yet how many electronic devices loaded with a zillion *"must have"* features do we own and use to their fullest, or even partial potential? Sex toys aside, I'm willing to bet few, if any.

Consider that, twenty years after their introduction, the majority of VCRs in America still blink perpetual noontime; we scramble to upgrade our computers for ones with more features, more power, more bonus programs, while continuing to use only a tiny fraction of their functionality and capability; and for all the home alarm systems sold with multiple features, zones, and timers, despite spending large sums for such systems, most owners simply turn the perimeter alarm on before heading out, if they remember at all, once the novelty has worn off.

In the Information Age version of "keeping up with the Joneses," the more features and "things" we acquire, the more complete we feel as people, even if we only use a fraction of what we've paid for.

But this corporate-fed lust for technology is just another national addiction with potential long-term consequences.

For starters, let's look at the American cell phone phenomenon.

Believe it or not, my main reason for owning one is not to impress friends with fancy ring tones, designer casings, or having it serve as a pocket organizer, alarm clock, Internet browser, e-mail client, stock trader, and personal entertainment center when I'm not at my desk — I own a cellular phone for one major reason: to place and receive phone calls. What the ringer sounds like or what kind of games and screensavers I can download is of no concern to me.

While cell phone purchasers are being inundated with television advertisements and discounts for new cell phones that can SMS, handle Instant Messages and zap small photos from one phone to another, I just want one that can carry a call decently. A discreet beep or two is more than sufficient to alert me I've got an incoming call; a polyphonic ring tone of the

William Tell Overture is not only unnecessary but probably damn annoying to the people around me.

It's not that all the gee-whiz features being thrown into today's cell phones couldn't be fun — it's just that until my cell phone network carrier can guarantee that I will be able to receive and place calls indoors, outdoors, underground, while moving or standing still, horizontally or vertically, while my television is turned on or off, and anywhere I am in the country, they can keep their new features. When my cell phone service is as reliable as my home phone service, I'll be happy to listen to their upgrade sales pitches.

Another example of this techno-lust can be found at home, with the next generation of kitchen appliances.

No longer content to simply keep our cold foods cold and frozen foods frozen, we're seeing refrigerators that can alert us via e-mail when the milk expires or that the ten-day-old Thai chicken has started growing furry legs in its container and is making sexual advances on last night's leftover Peking duck.

The day I welcome an e-mail message from an appliance telling me to bring home a quart of milk is the day I will commit myself for psychological help — because despite being in the prime of my life, I'm obviously too disabled to remember my own name or other routine facets of my personal life. And that's quite a poor condition to be in.

Appliances aside, let's consider another, more serious, issue associated with our infatuation with technology, and one that directly impacts anyone owning or using a personal computer and embracing the many benefits of the Information Age.

What will happen to the stored digital information of today?

The majority of documents used and created today such as books, letters, and papers are written using commercial computer software like Microsoft Word or WordPerfect. Quantitative analysis is presented in Microsoft Excel spreadsheets or Corel Quattro. Large databases run on Oracle or Microsoft Access systems. E-mail is stored in any number of proprietary formats, depending on what e-mail program you or your company use. The goofy, lukewarm idea of electronic books — those that are available — are released in proprietary, secret formats developed by commercial entities like Adobe and Microsoft.

Unfortunately, nearly all of today's mainstream computer software shares one dangerous quality: they're often proprietary technologies developed by commercial entities and designed to work only on a specific set of computer systems for a specific length of time before becoming obsolete, either by failure or by the release of newer products that deliberately won't support older technology.

Sadly, nobody thinks about these long-term ramifications, choosing instead to climb aboard the upgrade bandwagon and blindly embracing the latest-and-greatest thing as soon as they're released. Sometimes they're forced to — especially if their existing stuff won't work with newer technology — but more often than not, upgrades are forced on customers by companies trying to turn a continual profit and ensure a long-term relationship with, and dependence by, their customers.

This is very dangerous thing.

When Microsoft released its Word 97 product, it quietly changed the file format that its word processor, Microsoft Word, used to save documents. Users of earlier versions of Microsoft Word wishing to exchange documents with users of Word 97 had to purchase expensive upgrades to facilitate this critical and quite simple business process.

Clearly, Microsoft was trying to leverage its marketplace dominance in the word processing software and operating systems market by forcing users to pay more to continue accessing documents they created.[92] Fortunately, Microsoft quietly responded to poignant customer protests and enabled Word 97 to be fully compatible with earlier versions, and vice-versa, saving users from having to upgrade just to view documents created with a different version of the product.

Word 97 was an easily averted problem, but ask yourself this: will you be able to read memories contained in your high school diary, perhaps written in Microsoft Word, thirty years from now? What if your future version of Word isn't backwards-compatible, or the format of your data file isn't forward-compatible with a similar product available at the time? What will you do when you can't revisit your memories — not because *you* can't read them, but because there's nothing available to read them with, or because they're electronically "locked" to your old computer? What about the gigabytes of music in your MP3 collection? How will you enjoy today's music in the distant future?

The same problem will exist for the reams of saved e-mail, legal forms, and tax documents you amass over time, especially when it involves documents generated by programs that are "locked" to a specific computer, something that is becoming increasingly more common in today's commercial software packages.[93]

In the case of electronic books, will material published today in Adobe's E-Reader format and stored in digital libraries be readable in 2030? For that matter, will Adobe even be around then? Will the hard drives, CDs, or DVDs containing this information be accessible by the computers of 2030? If Adobe's not around, what provisions are in place for the information contained in years of e-Reader books to be made available to the public? How will that occur? Or is that information — those collected products of human society — destined for obscurity?

Vendors, governments, and customers need to realize that just because something is no longer part of a business plan doesn't mean it's not still important to the world. If there are people using older products that are no longer part of the vendor's future business strategy, the vendor should release the product to the world free of charge, and back into what prominent techno-lawyer Larry Lessig calls the *"Creative Commons."* No technical support from the vendor is needed — the enterprising community of global geeks will work to resolve any problems that may arise down the road, but such actions will help individuals who require ongoing access to now-obsolete data and applications.

This is a problem that business, government, and common sense must remedy for the public interest. However, first we must overcome our infatuation with technology and corporate greed long enough to realize the long-term problems and dependencies we're inflicting on ourselves by continuing to lock our information into proprietary technologies owned by commercial entities more interested in making a profit than enhancing the good of society's future.

Technology isn't supposed to be an enabler of forgetfulness; it should enable a person's efficiency and help her or him become a more, not less, independent, capable, and enlightened individual. Continually rushing out to buy the latest-and-greatest gadget or upgrade to the next version of something – either voluntarily or involuntarily — won't necessarily help you reach that goal, despite what we're led to believe by the corporate marketing folks hawking their wares. Not to mention, why rush out to purchase something you're not going to use to its fullest capability? Besides, do you really use every feature or function in every piece of technology or software that you own?

Relinquishing the task of frequently exercising your memory and letting technology remember routine things for you while still in the prime of your life isn't beneficial, it's setting you up for a long-term dependency on something that might (and generally does) fail down the road, be it a company or nifty gadget. And being unable to access old data because a corporation no longer makes decades-old software available is setting us up for a data- and memory-retrieval fiasco.

But by then, your own memory will be too far gone to help you, so you're truly out of luck.

Unless you've decided to upgrade before then, that is.

20

Hollywood's War For Social Control

Our Age of Anxiety is, in great part, the result of trying to do today's jobs with yesterday's tools.
   - Marshall McLuhan

In July 2002, nineteen American legislators sent Attorney General John Ashcroft a letter urging him to devote more Justice Department resources to fight computer users swapping digital entertainment media without permission.[94] In other words, nineteen members of Congress sat down and composed a letter — or, more likely the entertainment industry's Washington lobbyists wrote a letter and these members of Congress signed it in exchange for considerable donations to their reelection fund — asking the head of our Justice Department to allocate more FBI time and energy to try and stop Jane and John Doe from copying and sharing music, films and video games among friends or family.

Now try and forget for a moment that the FBI is neck-deep in several internal crises of confidence and competence, having a hard time recruiting and keeping qualified agents, and quickly shifting from a stand-alone, diverse federal law enforcement agency into an entity trying to successfully counter the emerging threats of terrorism in America.

According to the Recording Industry Association of America (RIAA), the Motion Picture Association of America (MPAA), and their paid-for legislators, none of this really matters much in the grand scheme of things. What matters is

American entertainment — who controls it and who gets to distribute it.

In other words the enforcement of commercial copyrights on music and movies should be on a near-equal footing to tracking down international terrorists.

This argument is made all the more palatable when "peer-to-peer" — a valuable technological architecture — is interpreted and subsequently marketed by the RIAA and MPAA in hysterical press releases, testimony to Congress, and on talk shows as synonymous with illegal "pirating" (sharing) of their product and the cause of potential economic terrorism against the $40 billion entertainment industry, even though Hollywood had a record-breaking year for box-office profits in 2002.[95]

With this sort of hype, expect to see lobbyists pushing for a "War on File Sharing" to be added to the national "War" troika of the "War on Drugs," the "War on AIDS," and the "War on Terror."

Therefore, in the face of this industry hysteria, the question isn't how low they will sink to make a profit — this is the entertainment industry, after all — but why this such a hot topic for scholars, technologists, and the entertainment industry itself?

To answer the questioning in a word: fear. The entertainment industry is fearful of any new creative consumer technology that it doesn't exercise complete totalitarian control over.

Just think back some twenty some-odd years ago to the 1980s, when during Senate hearings, MPAA's President Jack Valenti flew into a semi-psychotic fit as he equated the potential danger to the entertainment industry caused by consumer VCRs to the dangers presented to women by the Boston Strangler.[96] Of course, we now know that video sales and rentals are a major revenue source for the industry, but when it comes to embracing the future Jack, and the rest of the industry just can't seem to look into their crystal balls and see anything but a future of brimstone, hellfire, and Boston Stranglers.

As for the music side of the industry, declining album sales and profits have been blamed on peer-to-peer file sharing, internet webcasting, easily-shared .MP3 file formats, the easy availability of blank CDs and hard drives, and personal computers being shipped with CD burners as standard equipment. In fact, they'd pin their problems on just about anything except for themselves and their over-hyped — and oftentimes crappy — music that no one wants to pay good money to hear.[97]

For some reason that highly-educated and well-paid industry executives can't understand, saturating a market with look-alike/sound-alike teen bands will not drive fans to buy more CDs but rather allows one album to placate six differing bands fans, and thus save the industry some money by consolidating its talent and marketing budgets.[98] These same highly paid executives also forget that a federal court found RIAA member companies guilty of price-fixing CD sales during the 1990s, noting that during a decade when costs of nearly everything else declined, the price of new CDs actually climbed.[99]

But never mind the facts; it must be those darn CD burners in the PCs and casual copying between teenagers. As mentioned elsewhere in this book, it's the American Way to blame anything but ourselves and take responsibility for our problems. Hollywood's no different than anyone else in this regard.

Granted, organized international piracy groups (as opposed to sharing music casually between individuals or teenagers) has caused the music industry some economic damage, but I don't see major artists or studio executives standing on lines outside soup kitchens in Los Angeles or Seattle. And someone copying a CD under federal fair-use laws (a very complex topic made understandable by such outstanding books as Larry Lessig's *The Future of Ideas* and Jessica Littman's *Digital Copyright*) doesn't present a significant economic impact to the entertainment industry, either. If anything, casual and legal sharing of music helps broaden an artist's publicity and, if the product is good, it generates "buzz" and a level of marketing penetration Madison Avenue would envy.

Still, we see proposals to allow the entertainment industry to hack home computers so as to search and destroy[100] "illegally-copied" material; we hear the suggestion that all blank compact disks (and possibly hard drives) be taxed to compensate for piracy losses,[101] even if these items are used for backup of software and user's computer data and not for entertainment content. Worse yet, a proposal in 2002 by Senator Fritz "Hollywood" Hollings intended to require copyright enforcement "features" be part of *any* device capable of storing electronic data, from computers and DVD players or disks to microwaves, garage door openers, rectal thermometers, and more.[102]

The Hollings proposal — currently dead with the close of the 107th Congress and hopefully never to rise again — would have forced the interests of the $40 billion entertainment industry on the $500 billion-plus technology and hardware industries, and would have imposed draconian restrictions on an individual's use of technology, even for personal use. The flawed logic seems to be that unless *everything* that potentially could be used to facilitate copying is locked down, evil file sharing will abound and cause Hollywood significant economic losses.

Talk about the mouse trying to own the elephant herd.

Let's look at a few examples of what could happen if Hollywood gets its way. It could very well happen that while recording your family's antics on Christmas Eve, your new digital camcorder will shut down in the middle of filming your children playing in the living room because it detected a copyrighted television program being shown in the background, and you aren't *authorized* to record that program with that camcorder. Or you backup your new Avril Lavigne CD to your computer upstairs, but aren't allowed to copy it to your laptop, burn it onto a CD for the car, or use it anywhere else because the computer software (with built-in Hollywood control "features") has locked that data to one specific computer.[103] Maybe that CD you purchased can be played five times before it self-destructs or you purchase additional "plays" from the record company. Perhaps you purchase a DVD or record a television program for later viewing, only to find that you can't view it on more than one television. You'd be forced to buy multiple copies of music or movies in multiple formats, each with its own proprietary, clumsy way of ensuring that you can't fully enjoy what you pay for.

These recent legislative proposals show a belief that the only "creators" that should be allowed to easily bring new works to market — and thus the only ones who matter — are those under expensive contracts to the companies represented by their respective trade groups. So much for the garage band trying to establish itself independently[104] without a major record label's backing by using the Internet, personal computers, and store-bought blank CDs to produce and market their albums — *unless you've got the money to play by the cartel's rules, you just don't matter.*

This war for the control of information — and thus society — goes back to the early 1980s and the early years of the VCR and Jack Valenti's early public histrionics when Hollywood began a battle with the public and Congress to enact "Digital Rights Management" technologies to control the illegal distribution of its products. And though the public may not know it, much of how they use, and are expected to use, technology — from computers to DVD players — has been dictated by the profit-grubbing interests of the entertainment industry since then. It has gotten so bad that recent legislative proposals by those shilling for the entertainment industry have analysts referring publicly to these efforts as DRM — "*Digital Restrictions Management.*"

The most striking aspect of these recent Hollywood-centric legislative proposals — starting with the still-controversial Digital Millennium Copyright Act of 1998[105] — is that all of them automatically outlaws what *might* be done by someone and not what actually *is* done.[106]

American law is quite clear on the fact that simply knowing how to kill someone is not illegal, but committing murder is. However, under the current suite of Hollywood-centric laws, every person in America who knows how to kill someone would be arrested simply for knowing, regardless of whether they did anything with that knowledge or not. This type of law presumes a customer is guilty until they can be proven guiltier.

Having the potential to pirate software or entertainment material doesn't make everyone a criminal; rather, the industry and government needs to apply existing laws to catch the organized criminal groups that seriously impact Hollywood's profits instead of gunning for the legal, casual sharing between Joe and Jane after school, or an individual who wants to make a "mix" CD for the car.

It's a sure sign of obsessive-compulsive greed when the entertainment cartels are only too happy to lobby for laws and technologies[107] that presume every customer is a potential criminal while at the same time forcing them to purchase the same product repeatedly to use in the ways they're currently used to. This means potential new revenue streams for Hollywood, since it currently gets paid "only" once for a DVD or CD — when you purchase it — no matter how many times you use it, or how many friends borrow it from you.

In the future, while you might still purchase a physical item — such as a DVD or CD —it likely will come with a software-type license permitting you to use the item *only* in specific ways that are pre-authorized by the entertainment industry, such as what Universal Music introduced in 2001.[108] If Hollywood doesn't want you to watch that DVD or play that CD in a device not approved by its cartel's policies, you'll just have to buy another copy, or pay for the privilege. After all, you *might* be a criminal. True, I *could* be. But I'm not. And neither is most of the free world.

It's becoming clear that Hollywood's preferred ways of addressing its alleged piracy problems also will eliminate the privacy expectations of individuals. In the not-so-distant future, your computer may be forced to contact Microsoft (which sadly runs most consumer computers these days) or a third party copyright monitoring firm to verify that you paid for and are authorized to play that Avril Lavigne CD on a specific computer.

Sound crazy? It's already happening. In 2002, we learned that Microsoft was monitoring and recording what music and videos its Windows Media Player users were downloading to their computers.[109] If it's illegal for a video store owner to disclose what videos its patrons are renting,[110] why is it that Microsoft — and the entertainment industry — can do it? Do we really want a third party knowing our particular interests in movies and music? (Microsoft has since changed their policy, but they could always change it again.)

And though it's high time that the entertainment companies learn that if they treat their customers as criminals, they'll not only have fewer paying customers, but many more criminals to contend with, it's not the real issue at the heart of the copyright enforcement debate.

Despite all the hype about copyrights, royalties, and file sharing technology, we're forgetting is that *if you control the means to disseminate content, you can subsequently control the public.*

The real issue here is freedom: freedom of choice, and the freedom to create, distribute, and utilize digital information for any and all legal purposes.

Up until the concept of peer-to-peer file sharing technologies and the public Internet arrived in the late 1990s, the entertainment industry alone decided what artist or movie was supported, promoted, and published, and in what quantities. Technology born from the Information Age — such as peer-to-peer, personal CD burners, MP3 files, and the Internet in general — threatens to reverse this centralized control mechanism and profit stream, and enable anyone to publish and promote their content around the world while cutting the middleman — the RIAA and MPAA — out of the financial equation and creative management process.

Given the consolidation of media distribution outlets in 2003, if you can't afford, or are not willing, to play by the "established" means of information control, you are typically left to fend for yourself in local venues and audiences and rarely reach the broad markets controlled by the entertainment cartels, no matter how good your material is.

Thanks to the Information Age, this is not the case anymore. This harsh new reality terrifies the entertainment industry, who will in effect stop at nothing — no matter how ill conceived, shady, or what the chances are that it might come back to bite them later on — to keep its reign and control over a failing business model and changing economic and customer environment.

The copyright debate isn't only about profit, it's also about *who controls information*, and ultimately, *people and society*. That's the fundamental issue here.

And few, if any, are talking about it.

21

Empowering America – The Right Way

If you don't stand for something, you'll fall for anything.
— Malcom X

Believe it or not, despite what you may think at this point, I still love America; even though we've got a fair amount of problems cropping up that need to be *resolved*, not simply "addressed." If we ignore them, or fail to acknowledge them, it's no different than having that proverbial elephant in our living room, pretending that it's not really there and not really an elephant, either.

But that seems to be the recent trend for solving America's real problems. We all know about them, but few people want to talk about them. Politicians are afraid of offending any (or all) of the groups they need to count on for financing and votes; the general public has become disconnected and apathetic; various rights groups have become so narrowly focused and greedy that many have forgotten what they're lobbying for; few, if any, mainstream reporters are willing to face public retribution by filing stories that might offend advertisers or political figures; and the brave individuals who attempt to raise questions and point out potential problems are ridiculed on all fronts.

To counter this unfortunate trend, I will offer two suggestions on how a person can empower himself or herself and become a more responsible individual and capable American citizen. These are radical suggestions — but easily implemented, if you're willing to accept the challenge.

1. Think For (and Take Charge of) Yourself

Never allow yourself to be led along through life with blinders on. Be willing to do your own research and form your own opinions on things that matter to you, be it social policy, religion, national politics, or your choice of SUV, long-distance phone service, sexual orientation, or brand of toothpaste.

This is primarily accomplished by not obtaining all your information from a single source, and especially by *never* taking anything you hear as absolute truth. Since America's major news organizations are owned now by a handful of for-profit corporations, *news* becomes a product packaged to generate customers and profits and a place where it's next to impossible for people to separate information from opinion, and opinion from government-endorsed spin. Whether or not viewers become informed is of little interest as long as they stick around to watch the advertisements and buy whatever's being peddled.

Perhaps the best way to become a more informed person is to stay away from cable and network news programming and look for alternative sources of information. *Newshour with Jim Lehrer* is a product of the Public Broadcasting Service and an example of a traditional "hard news" program that does away with spinning logos and sinister music designed to captivate and entertain. One of *Newshour*'s key highlights are in-depth panel discussions on the news of the day with respected and established experts from government and academia. There's no shouting, bombast, or browbeating — multiple sides of an issue are presented and debated in a professional, distraction-free environment that enables viewers to make up their own minds after receiving more than a few short sound bytes. It's not always perfect, but *Newshour's* quality is light-years ahead of what you'll get from commercial news programs.

While PBS provides more thorough coverage of daily (*Newshour*) and weekly single-issue shows (*FrontLine*) than the commercial networks, you can always turn to public affairs channel C-SPAN for live unedited coverage of what key leaders say (and the audience reaction, which often is just as important as what's being said) and allows viewers to interpret what they see as they wish. There's no politically charged agenda and no network analysts commenting about what's on-screen and presenting simple, memorable sound bytes to the viewer. In other words, C-SPAN, not the FOX News Channel, truly epitomizes the marketing phrase "we report, you decide."

On the other hand, an alternative to purely American news or reporting is to search out news programs from overseas sources such as the BBC, ITN or SkyNews. These networks offer an excellent education on how the rest of the world perceives American news stories in addition to showing how the rest of the world interprets international events. Bolstering your American news programming — whatever it may be — with some foreign coverage will expand significantly your understanding of the critical issues of the day as reality, not a single network, corporation, or government, would show them. Many community public-access stations carry such programming each day.

Another source for international news and opinions are foreign-operated news websites and research centers — such as the Middle East Media Research Institute (MEMRI) or Agence France-Presse (AFP) — and independent news websites like Counterpunch.Org, Salon.Com, Truthout.Org, and others like them. These groups provide daily doses of relevant world news items and dissenting opinions that America's press won't touch with a ten-foot pole because it's just not *American enough* for its audience or too controversial for its advertisers. They do ask the tough questions about the issues affecting our lives and society, and deserve our thanks and support.

Media aside, you might consider how much emphasis you place on standards that you're asked to impose on yourself by organized religions, politicians, and the many organizations working on their behalf. Politicians, school administrators, students, and citizens alike must not allow themselves or their thinking to be subjugated by outdated philosophies, medieval religious dogma, corporate marketing spins, political pressure, or old-fashioned trickery. Empowering the individual means opening, not closing, their mind to new ideas and perspectives.

The lesson here is to *never* settle, and *never* be afraid to ask "why not" instead of only "why" as you explore new ideas or knowledge and expand your horizons. If something sounds strange, or suspicious, or you don't want to accept it, speak up! After all, you've got to stand for something, or you'll fall for anything — and it helps if you know what you're standing for in the first place.

Becoming more informed will help you think critically and ask questions about the world around you, since you'll start to see things as they really are instead of how others would like you to see them. At that point, it's up to you as a responsible citizen to make the effort to bring these concerns to public attention. Should you introduce items that the majority of your fellow citizens agree with, positive changes can be made to the status quo.

For example, in response to their concerns over the invasive surveillance powers of the USA PATRIOT Act that was passed after September 11, over one hundred local communities throughout America enacted symbolic — but still official — public referenda in an effort to draw enough public attention to this questionable law that the American citizenry at large will seek its reversal or redaction. Further, in a sign of local community solidarity and concern for the privacy of law-abiding American citizens — not to mention in defense of their professional integrity — some librarians create and distribute warning signs[111] alerting patrons that their reading habits might be under government scrutiny authorized by the USA PATRIOT Act, and the American Library Association even provides guidance on ensuring privacy of library users despite the new privacy-invading laws.[112] One Vermont bookstore even purges its customer lists to ensure the privacy of its patrons' reading interests if the American Brown Shirts (pardon me, federal agents operating under the USA-PATRIOT Act) come knocking.

These people and communities aren't unpatriotic — in a time of runaway government and carefully-crafted nationalist groupthink they're doing their *patriotic duty* by questioning and *peacefully challenging* what they believe is a dubious use of government powers without appropriate checks-and-balances. I commend them for their courage and efforts, and hope their efforts continue against the more draconian USA PATRIOT II law proposal being floated around Washington as this book goes to press. These groups must also work to ensure that such controversial new law enforcement powers - allegedly to combat terrorism – are used exclusively for that purpose and not extended to other, more mundane civil or criminal investigations; if so, these groups must take steps to alert the American public of the misuse of such secret government powers, lest America continue its patriotic transformation into a police state.

Edward R. Murrow, one of America's most respected journalists said, "We must not confuse dissent with disloyalty. When the loyal opposition dies, I think the soul of America dies with it." I hope we take his wisdom to heart in the months and years to come, especially as America faces new challenges to its national security.

2. Accept Personal Responsibility and Overcome The Politics of Ignorance

We've got to stop the national trend towards accepting praise while shirking responsibility, both on an organizational and personal level. Sure, it's uncomfortable, but if you make a mistake, it's better to be honest about it than scramble to cover it up or blame others. Those who choose to blame others for their own actions, no matter how wealthy or politically powerful, are humanity at its worst, and should be seen for what they really are. People like Bernie Ebbers (Worldcom), Ken Lay (Enron), Cardinal Bernard Law (Catholic Church), Scott Sullivan (Worldcom), Bob Torricelli (US Senate), Bernie Schwartz (Loral Systems) and Martha Stewart (ImClone) are just some examples that come to mind.

If you're a parent, *be* a parent, and don't outsource your natural responsibilities to third parties. If you're a school administrator, prepare your students for the future to be fully functioning members of adult society instead of mindless, drug-addicted drones devoid of ambition and the will (or ability) to think for themselves.

If you spill a cup of coffee on your lap while driving down the road, it's *your* fault for being clumsy, rather than negligence by the restaurant or maker of the car's cup-holder. If your child accidentally shoots someone with your gun, it's *your* fault for not properly securing the weapon and teaching your child gun safety, not the fault of the gun maker for failing to include a childproof trigger lock. If you're a Catholic Bishop, have the courage to take responsibility for disciplining *your* troublemakers instead of drop-shipping them to another branch office to escape punishment or controversy. If you're an elected official, stand up for the interests of *your* constituents and America as a whole, instead of fearing reprisals by special interests who don't care one whit about the good of your constituents or America. It's depressing — and hypocritical — to see our national and corporate leaders preaching accountability time and again, only to be caught doing the exact opposite themselves. Indeed, *they* listened to the lessons of marketing genius P.T. Barnum when he rightly said, "There's a sucker born every minute." We should, too.

We must remember that nothing is more appealing to the established organizations of social control than masses of people who are happy to roll over and accept whatever's presented to them, like good little brainwashed sheep. If in doubt, just remember that Congress and the majority of America did nothing while the second Bush administration proceeded to rewrite large portions of the Constitution and grant governmental agencies broad — and in some cases, excessive — powers of surveillance, arrest, detention, profiling, and privacy invasion, all under the feel-good guise of "protecting the American Homeland" contained in the USA PATRIOT Act. Invoking the memory of September 11 soon became the standard emotion-filled technique to ensure that legislation of all sorts was passed quickly regardless of how much — or even if — it related to terrorism, and people bought it — hook, line, and sinker.

Americans still don't realize (or don't care) how their lives are shaped by corporate and religious interests seeking to impose their special needs and desires on the public and at the public's expense. From abortion rights to gun control, what children are taught in school and how people use the latest technology, the majority of people don't monitor these issues until they're passed into law and it affects them in some new way they don't agree with — at which point it's too late to change them. They just continue living their lives in blissful ignorance while facilitating America's decline into a world of diminishing possibilities and alternatives for the future, creating what American philosopher Henry David Thoreau called "a life of quiet desperation" and *The Matrix* character Morpheus called "a prison for your mind."

At which point, special-interest groups will smile and know they've won another victory for themselves at the expense of the public — and America's vaunted democracy will continue its transformation into a muted oligarchy while American citizens will become less capable (and relevant) in determining what constitutes *their* cherished American culture.

So, if you're a proud American citizen, take personal responsibility for your actions and for holding our society's leaders accountable for theirs. It's not only our responsibility as people; but in the latter case, at least for now, as citizens, it's *still* our democratic right!

Thanks for reading.

Afterward

As this book goes to press in July 2003, I am saddened to report that nothing has changed for the better since I first started researching this book in mid-2001. Not that I expected much, but it would've been nice – and bolstered my faith in our modern society – to delete or modify some of my comments and observations appearing in the manuscript. Oh, well. We can always hope.

Right now, it's been three months since the United States "liberated" Iraq — and despite the presence of nearly 150,000 troops (three times more than the Administration proposed to use) there's no sign of the vaunted weapons of mass destruction that so terrified the Bush and Blair administrations. More American troops have been killed since President Bush triumphantly declared the "end of major combat operations" after his staged photo-op landing aboard an aircraft carrier than during "major combat operations" — forcing the Pentagon to respond to (and ultimately confirm) accusations that Iraq is becoming an unconventional, guerilla-type wartime environment very reminiscent of Vietnam, particularly as the body count of Americans killed or injured is reported to the public each evening on the nightly news.

Of course, it was easy to win the combat part of war, but they're finding it's much more difficult to win the follow-on peace. But, when you go into war based primarily on politicized intelligence, the advice of defectors who have their own ambitions, refusing to listen to the advice of your military leaders, and no Plan B, this is not an entirely unexpected outcome.

Yet, while the American public is becoming more frustrated with the cost in lives and dollars with our Iraq endeavor little is being done officially to hold the administration accountable for its actions leading us to this very troubling politico-military situation; the Administration, along with its Republican lackeys in Congress, is stone-walling attempts to investigate pre-war intelligence analysis and the ever-changing reasons to invade Iraq seemingly for no other reason than to shield the President and their political party from embarrassment going into the 2004 elections. This is happening despite several senior career government officials – ambassadors and intelligence analysts – stating publicly the serious concerns within the intelligence community over how the Administration presented and politicized intelligence findings before launching (and selling to the world) a war in Iraq.

Every Administration has its noteworthy "spins" and cover-ups that historians will always associate with its legacy – and this definitely is one for the history books. Historians will argue for years about what's worse for America's security and perception around the world: a president who lies about his personal sex life (and gets impeached as a result) or one who scrambles to find, finesse, or fabricate enough reasons - real or perceived - to go to war and blatantly ignore the international system unless it suits his plans. (Who's the revisionist now, Mister Bush?)

Our government continues exercising its controversial self-proclaimed imperial right of military pre-emption in the name of national security and international hegemony. Our military is still involved in Afghanistan (yes, we're still there even though the media doesn't report on it much anymore) Iraq, and continuing to eyeball North Korea and Iran as the next places likely to experience America's pre-emption strategy – with or without the support or endorsement of the international community, of course.

On the home front, the American economy is still in the gutter, with a $455 billion dollar federal budget deficit for 2003 (50% more than the White House projected only five months earlier) and unemployment statistics for June 2003 are at about 6.4 percent (the highest point in ten years) according to the Department of Labor. Of course, we're still running up a $4 billion-a-month tab to support long-term military operations in Iraq and Afghanistan, and who knows how much more we'll be spending on foreign military ventures in the future as America flexes its preemptive muscles. Perhaps the Administration believes if it can keep the news media focused on the action-packed overseas activities associated with its "War on Terror" they won't be so quick to report on other more important (but politically embarrassing) issues here at home. After all, any solutions to our current economic problems (many of which were caused or exacerbated by the Bush Administration) will run contradictory to the President's 2003 State of The Union message when he emphatically promised that "...we will not pass along our problems to other Congresses, to other presidents and other generations." How this domestic economic mess will be cleared up *completely* during his term of office is anyone's guess; unless a miracle happens, future generations almost certainly will be affected by the economic masturbation going on today.

We're also seeing American politics sink to an all-time low in Washington. In mid-July, Republican Bill Thomas, the acerbic chairman of the House Ways and Means Committee, called the Capitol Police to round up Democrat members of the committee who adjourned to the committee's library to review a pension overhaul bill (coincidentally numbered "HR 1776") they were to consider but had not been given ample time to review prior to the vote, having only received it late into the previous night. Despite the presence of a lone Democrat – Pete Stark – remaining in the room to prevent a unanimous consent vote by the Republican majority, Thomas called for, and received the requisite number of votes to pass the bill out of Committee unilaterally; essentially ignoring Stark's parliamentary objection to block the vote on behalf of the Democrat minority. Name-calling between committee members followed.

The fight spilled over to the House Chamber on that otherwise quiet summer Friday afternoon, where members began to accuse the other party of political games on a level rarely seen in recent years. Minority Leader Nancy Pelosi offered – and failed – to win House support for a resolution condemning Thomas' action and negating the Committee's unilateral vote. Likewise, House Speaker Dennis Hastert failed to reach a compromise between the two parties. Granted, there are any number of "dirty tricks" that can be played in Congress when considering legislation, but not playing by your own rules and completely ignoring the minority party isn't one of them, particularly on a bill that *had* strong support from the minority party! Many in the House, including several Republicans, felt embarrassed and saddened by the day's events. As well they should. They embarrassed America that day. (Note: Days later, Thomas delivered a tearful face — and (hopefully) GOP-saving apology in front of the assembled House.)

Many states continue to sink into deeper financial trouble but are receiving little help or support from the federal government, even as they struggle to meet federally-mandated homeland security initiatives. Despite the Administration's frequent public praise for "America's Heroes" – our police, fire, and rescue personnel – many are being fired to cut costs. And, given that money is tight, especially for training and new equipment, those who would respond to a potential terrorist attack are woefully unprepared to do so successfully despite the best wishes of and patriotic rhetoric from politicians back in Washington. These comments were echoed in the findings of the chilling Council on Foreign Relations report from July 2003 entitled *Emergency Responders: Drastically Underfunded, Dangerously Unprepared*. Of course, the

Administration and its Congressional lackeys dismissed these independent findings and recommendations as "excessive" or "impractical" but many emergency responders and terrorism analysts strongly disagree.

The government continues to fund and support "Homeland Security" programs and laws that invade the privacy of law-abiding citizens and have the potential to turn the freedom-loving United States into a massive surveillance state complete with secretive police powers. According to a Justice Department report released in mid-2003, the controversial USA PATRIOT Act designed to support terrorism investigations has been extended to non-terrorism-related cases, including kidnapping, extortion, and fraud. While not entirely unexpected, confirming these abuses of power took place represents a fundamental shift in the emphasis our government places on the cherished American values of freedom and personal privacy, challenges the accountability and integrity of our elected officials, and questions the commitment of such officials in preserving the core values of our great nation.

As you read this, several states are enacting laws to restrict the sale of violent videogames to teenagers, saying that it's these games responsible for youth violence. There's even talk of a national law to prohibit the sale of such games to underage kids. Yet nowhere are parents and educators being held accountable for their actions (or inactions) as role models for future generations. In fairness, if such laws are passed, Congress and state legislators must also enact laws prohibiting anyone under 18 from watching the local, national, or international news, reading newspapers, or surfing the Internet, since it's obvious there's more real-world violence presented in these mediums than in a video game. Otherwise, as with so many other policies, it's lawmakers and special-interest groups doing what they do best – sticking their heads in the sand and avoiding any attempt to fix the underlying cause of national problems.

The American news media still provides "info-tainment" for the masses, most recently in its reality-television coverage of the Jessica Lynch "ordeal" and her (coincidentally) Pentagon-videotaped "rescue" from an Iraqi hospital. Fortunately, as the facts are becoming known despite the Pentagon's reluctance to release unedited video of the event, the media (including FOX News) had to correct and tone down its patriotic, "feel-good" coverage of this controversial story. Unfortunately, thanks to the media continuing to serve as the unelected voice of the government, most Americans still think Saddam Hussein played a major part in the attacks of September 11 despite any hard evidence supporting that theory; and nobody's asking any questions about this dubious connection and why it's received so much national attention. Accuracy? A "sacred public duty" to inform the public and ask the "tough" questions? Hah! You forget — their primary goal is to keep advertisers happy and profits rolling. Anything else is not part of the business plan.

The National Assessment of Educational Progress (the nation's 'report card' on education quality) released its 2002 report, noting that while elementary school students notably improved their writing and analytical abilities, half of America's graduating high school seniors still can't express a coherent set of thoughts or write beyond a "basic" level of competency and quality. The report cites "disorganized self-expression or Internet chat" as a major obstacle for students and teachers to overcome. Here's a clear-cut example of technology's popularity and casual means of communication serving as a detriment to personal skills development. Certainly, technology has its place in education and society, but its use should not detract from or replace teaching and assessing the fundamental skills necessary for a person to function in the world as a capable adult.

On the technology front, intellectual property "rights" continue to be the single greatest legal and policy issue around the world. Despite some congressmen proposing rational and acceptable solutions to the issue, we continue seeing "shoot-first" proposals including levying outlandish fines or jail time on people casually trading music and the goofy (but fortunately impossible) desire to "remotely destroy or disable" the computers of people suspected of (but not necessarily proven to be) pirating music. In this area, we're continuing to see individuals viewed as potential criminals and treated as guilty until proven guiltier by the unelected members of the entertainment industry's greedy cartels. The head of the international police consortium InterPol even claimed that the pirating of music and movies over the Internet is becoming the preferred method of funding terrorist groups – but failed to offer any evidence supporting his claim. Here's a clear-cut case of "fighting terrorism" being invoked in a non-terrorism-related legal issue in the hopes that the mere mention of "terrorism" will curry public support for a flawed policy position and industry strategy. And, the RIAA has sent nearly a thousand subpoenas to federal court in recent days targeting people they *believe* are illegally pirating music on the Internet. Its goal, apparently, is to overwhelm the courts with enough complaints against individuals to force court officers to complain about their increased workload – and give a sympathetic (and paid-for-by-the-RIAA) Congress a reason to enact further RIAA-friendly, anti-creative, anti-consumer legislation. Expect RIAA donations to certain members of Congress to increase in 2004.

Recently, another installment of the world's favorite wizard — young Harry Potter – was released to adoring fans worldwide. And, true to form, there were book burnings, protests, and statements of condemnation from the Religious Right who continued preaching that such fantasy adventures are evil since they promote the acknowledgement of something supernatural other than the Christian God.

In a landmark decision, the Supreme Court of the United States ruled that what happens in a bedroom between two consenting adults – who happen to be of the same sex – is not a matter of government interest, and that such people deserve to practice their consenting sexuality with the same privacy that heterosexual couples have enjoyed for years. Of course, the Religious Right reacted as if this was a personal ruling from Satan that signaled the end of morality in America, and two Senators – Republicans Bill Frist and Rick Santorum – obviously catering to America's religious zealots, are floating the idea of attempting to pass a Constitutional amendment to prohibit anything but heterosexual marriage and sexual relations, since in their faith-based eyes, such activities are not only "immoral" but "criminal." The religious industry's response was equally nuts – zealot leaders from the mainstream Religious Right launched public campaigns urging their followers to pray for 'God' to "put it in the minds of these three judges [voting in the majority on the sodomy decision] that the time has come to retire [and be replaced by conservatives catering to the Religious Right who won't vote against us in the future.]"

Forget the refreshing fact that human society's values might be evolving (and becoming more open-minded and tolerant) after centuries of dogmatic thinking and aggressive intolerance. No, the *status quo* must be maintained, because that's what these folks think their particular "God" wants — social evolution or competing beliefs be damned. How dare human evolution interfere with these group's dogmatic views and ability to impress their views on the rest of the *infidel* world?

The bottom line is that as this book goes to press, America's culture and world standing is deteriorating with each passing week as our great nation continues to spiral out of control, both domestically and internationally.

America's culture was changing even before September 2001. Granted, change occurs naturally and is an expected constant in the universe. However, in recent years, the speed and impact of the changes to American society increased and became much more disturbing to those citizens concerned about what our American ideals stand for in the world and here at home.

I guess it's true — the more things change, the more they stay the same. And in the political arena, that's not only depressing, but a very sad state of affairs. What that means for our future is anyone's guess; but sadly, given current conditions, I'm not optimistic. I sincerely hope to be proven wrong.

I've got no regrets that – thanks to my friends, teachers, colleagues, mentors, and parents – I see the world for what is and not how others would like me to see it to satisfy their own purposes and niche desires. It may not always be pretty, and I may not always like what I see, but at least it's reality, and I can act accordingly on matters that concern me.

The bottom line is that this approach makes me a stronger person and more capable citizen able to make a positive difference in the future of our great country and cherished American culture.

We should all be so fortunate. And willing.

Endnotes

Web-based links to sources cited in this book were accurate at press time. In some cases where news stories are in pay-for-view archives, to accommodate readers wishing to access them, I have attempted to locate alternate sites where readers can find such stories in their entirety. However, as is the nature of the Internet, these sites are subject to change without warning. So don't say I didn't warn you.

Notes For Chapter 1

1. http://www.mirror.co.uk/news/allnews/page.cfm?objectid=12713155&method=full&siteid=50143

Notes For Chapter 2

2. http://www.nbc.com/nbc/The_Tonight_Show_with_Jay_Leno/jaywalking/

3. Report cited in this Washington Times article reprinted at: http://www.deepscience.com/articles/usa_science.html.

4. Statistics cited in a Christian Science Monitor article from November 2001. Article available at http://www.csmonitor.com/2001/1102/p11s2-coop.html

5. The press release (with a link to the study) is available from ACTA at http://www.goacta.org/press/Press%20Releases/2-16-00PR.htm

6. The press release (with a link to the study) is available from the National Geographic at http://www.nationalgeographic.com/events/releases/pr021120.html

7. http://www.usafreedomcorps.gov/for_volunteers/vsap/youth_achievement.asp

8. http://usinfo.state.gov/admin/005/wwwh1m08.html.

9. http://www.accessatlanta.com/ajc/business/cnn/1202/27warontv.html.

10. http://query.nytimes.com/search/article-page.html?res=9502E1DC1139F93AA35754C0A960958260.

11. http://www.worldpress.org/Europe/920.cfm

12. http://www.aberdeennews.com/mld/aberdeennews/news/nation/5223562.htm.

13. http://www.whitehouse.gov/news/releases/2001/09/20010926-5.html#BillMaher-Comments.

14. http://judiciary.senate.gov/testimony.cfm?id=121&wit_id=42.

15. http://www.cnn.com/2003/US/Northeast/03/05/offbeat.peace.arrest.reut/index.html

16. Cited by media-watcher Norm Solomon in his March 2002 column appearing at http://www.fair.org/media-beat/020307.html

17. Term favored by the George W. Bush administration during its first year in office.

18. Check out the top left side of http://www.whitehouse.gov/

19. This relates to the idea of "Newspeak' appearing in George Orwell's Politics and the English Language, as related to his Big Brother Groupthinking Society of 1984.

Notes For Chapter 3

20. Again, it's very much like George Orwell predicted.

Notes For Chapter 4

21. http://www.metroactive.com/papers/sonoma/01.09.97/walmart-music-9702.html

22. Ibid.

23. http://www.freedomforum.org/templates/document.asp?documentID=15820.

24. http://www.smh.com.au/articles/2002/11/15/1037080920105.html.

25. http://www.wealthpreserve.com/www/articles/asset_protection/Could_You_Lose_All_You_Own.htm

26. http://www.sptimes.com/News/100400/Business/The_most_frivolous_la.shtml.

27. Ibid.

28. Ibid.

29. http://www.power-of-attorneys.com/stupid_lawsuit_detail.asp?stupid_ID=22.

30. http://www.calahouston.org/best98.html.

31. http://www.nationalcenter.org/LB13.html (cites the Los Angeles Times)

32. http://abcnews.go.com/sections/us/DailyNews/fatsuit020725.html.

33. Ibid.

Notes For Chapter 5

34. http://www.signonsandiego.com/news/metro/danielle/20020917-9999_1n17news.html.

35. http://www.napa.ufl.edu/2002news/sharks02.htm.

Notes For Chapter 6

36. http://www.cga.state.ct.us/coc/bullying_task_force_report%20updated.htm.

Notes For Chapter 7

37. http://www.wpmi.com/Global/story.asp?S=1138542.

38. http://www.examiner.net/stories/041802/ope_041802023.shtml.

39. http://www.ncac.org/cen_news/cn72long_short.html.

40. http://archive.aclu.org/news/2000/n112100b.html.

41. http://www.freedomforum.org/templates/document.asp?documentID=10777.

42. http://news.com.com/2100-1023-214998.html?legacy=cnet.

43. http://www.freedomforum.org/templates/document.asp?documentID=13082.

44. http://www.splc.org/newsflash.asp?id=297.

Notes For Chapter 8

45. http://advancement.sdsu.edu/marcomm/news/clips/Archive/Jan2003/010203/010203parents.html

46. http://www.drivehomesafe.com/control_teendriver_speeding_driverlicense2.htm.

47. http://www.comcast.com/Support/Corp1/FAQ/FaqDetail_81.html.

48. http://www.thejournalnews.com/newsroom/010503/E1bcparents.html.

Notes For Chapter 9

49. http://www.ed.gov/Technology/comm-mit.html.

50. http://www.cnn.com/2002/TECH/fun.games/09/21/playstationhomework/.

51. http://www.siliconvalley.com/mld/siliconvalley/5004120.htm.

Notes For Chapter 10

52. http://www.researchprotection.org/infomail/0802/14.html.

53. http://www.cnn.com/2001/HEALTH/parenting/08/29/ritalin.schools/index.html.

54. http://www.census.gov/prod/2001pubs/c2kbr01-12.pdf.

55. http://www.phillyburbs.com/couriertimes/kidsincrisis/stories/0506ritalin.shtml.

Notes For Chapter 13

56. http://www.usatoday.com/travel/columnist/business/woodyard/woodyard12.htm.

57. http://www.washingtonpost.com/ac2/wp-dyn?pagename=article&node=&contentId=A61430-2002Oct21&notFound=true.

58. http://www.smh.com.au/text/articles/2002/12/27/1040511177274.htm.

59. http://gazette.unc.edu/archives/02sep11/file.4.html

60. http://www.unc.edu/chan/speech_archive/npcspeech_8_2002.html.

61. http://www.dailytarheel.com/vnews/display.v/ART/2002/08/20/3d623ea97b622

62. http://www.post-gazette.com/regionstate/20010326bookburn2.asp.

63. http://news.bbc.co.uk/1/hi/entertainment/arts/1735623.stm.

64. http://www.eonline.com/News/Items/0,1,10431,00.html.

Notes For Chapter 14

65. http://safety.fhwa.dot.gov/community/srlr_launch.htm.

66. http://www.freedom.gov/auto/news/truth.asp.

67. Ibid.

68. Ibid.

69. Ibid.

70. http://www.washtimes.com/metro/20020927-4563013.htm.

71. http://www.thesandiegochannel.com/sand/news/stories/news-79680220010530-180541.html.

72. http://www.speedtrap.org/stetlaws.htm#Texas%20Law.

73. http://www.hwysafety.org/support.htm.

74. http://safety.fhwa.dot.gov/community/srlr_media.htm.

Notes For Chapter 15

75. http://www.cnn.com/2001/TRAVEL/NEWS/12/18/airport.shutdown/?related

76. http://seattletimes.nwsource.com/html/localnews/134609869_webseatac05.html.

77. http://www.tsa.gov/public/display?content=164.

78. http://www.tsa.gov/public/display?content=115.

79. http://www.tsa.gov/public/interapp/editorial/editorial_0598.xml.

80. http://news.bbc.co.uk/2/hi/americas/1769191.stm.

81. http://www.politechbot.com/p-04169.html.

82. http://www.nytimes.com/2002/11/14/opinion/14SAFI.html.

83. http://www.sfgate.com/cgi-bin/article.cgi?f=/c/a/2003/03/10/MN14634.DTL.

84. http://www.ala.org/alaorg/oif/fbiinyourlibrary.html.

85. http://www.sftt.org/dwa/2002/12/18/3.html.

Notes For Chapter 16

86. http://www.partnershipforpublicwarning.org/ppw/docs/11_25_2002report.pdf.

87. http://www.guardian.co.uk/usa/story/0,12271,897875,00.html.

Notes For Chapter 18

88. http://www.foxnews.com/story/0,2933,41351,00.html.

89. http://www.cbsnews.com/stories/2002/08/27/national/main519931.shtml.

90. http://www.cbsnews.com/stories/2002/09/11/september11/main521521.shtml.

Notes For Chapter 19

91. http://www.spectrum.ieee.org/INST/jan98/pres_col.html.

92. http://www.chicagotribune.com/technology/chi-021105himowitz,0,5341740.story?coll=chi-technology-hed.

93. http://news.com.com/2100-1017-979357.html.

Notes For Chapter 20

94. http://news.com.com/2100-1023-949229.html?tag=mainstry.

95. http://enquirer.com/editions/2002/12/31/biz_movierecord31.html.

96. A copy of his testimony is available at http://cryptome.org/hrcw-hear.htm.

97. http://www.musicjournal.org/01cdsales.htm.

98. http://www.sltrib.com/2002/jun/06092002/business/743868.htm.

99. http://news.com.com/2100-1023-960183.html.

100. http://news.com.com/2100-1023-946316.html.

101. http://www.wired.com/news/politics/0,1283,50995,00.html.

102. http://www.politechbot.com/docs/cbdtpa/hollings.s2048.032102.html.

103. http://www.cl.cam.ac.uk/~rja14/tcpa-faq.html.

104. http://www.wired.com/news/digiwood/0,1412,55926,00.html.

105. http://www.eff.org/IP/DMCA/hr2281_dmca_law_19981020_pl105-304.html

106. http://www.eff.org/IP/DMCA/20020503_dmca_consequences.html.

107. http://news.com.com/2100-1023-277197.html?legacy=cnet.

108. http://www.musichelponline.com/legal/.

109. http://www.internetnews.com/dev-news/article.php/10_978251.

110. http://www.epic.org/privacy/vppa/.

Notes For Chapter 21

111. http://www.librarian.net/technicality.html.

112. http://www.ala.org/Content/NavigationMenu/Our_Association/Offices/ALA_Washington/Issues2/Civil_Liberties,_Intellectual_Freedom,_Privacy/The_USA_Patriot_Act_and_Libraries/The_USA_Patriot_Act_and_Libraries.htm.

About The Author

Although holding undergraduate and graduate degrees in international relations, Richard Forno's career has been focused on keeping hackers out of computer networks. Co-author of two books on computer security (*The Art of Information Warfare* and *Incident Response*) and a popular techno-political commentator and lecturer, he's known for taking an understandable and unconventional — some would say heretical — view on the world, constantly challenging audiences to interpret reality by thinking for themselves on matters of importance. This is his first non-geek book.

Richard lives in the Washington, DC area.

www.rickonline.org

Printed in the United States
1284300001B/4-9